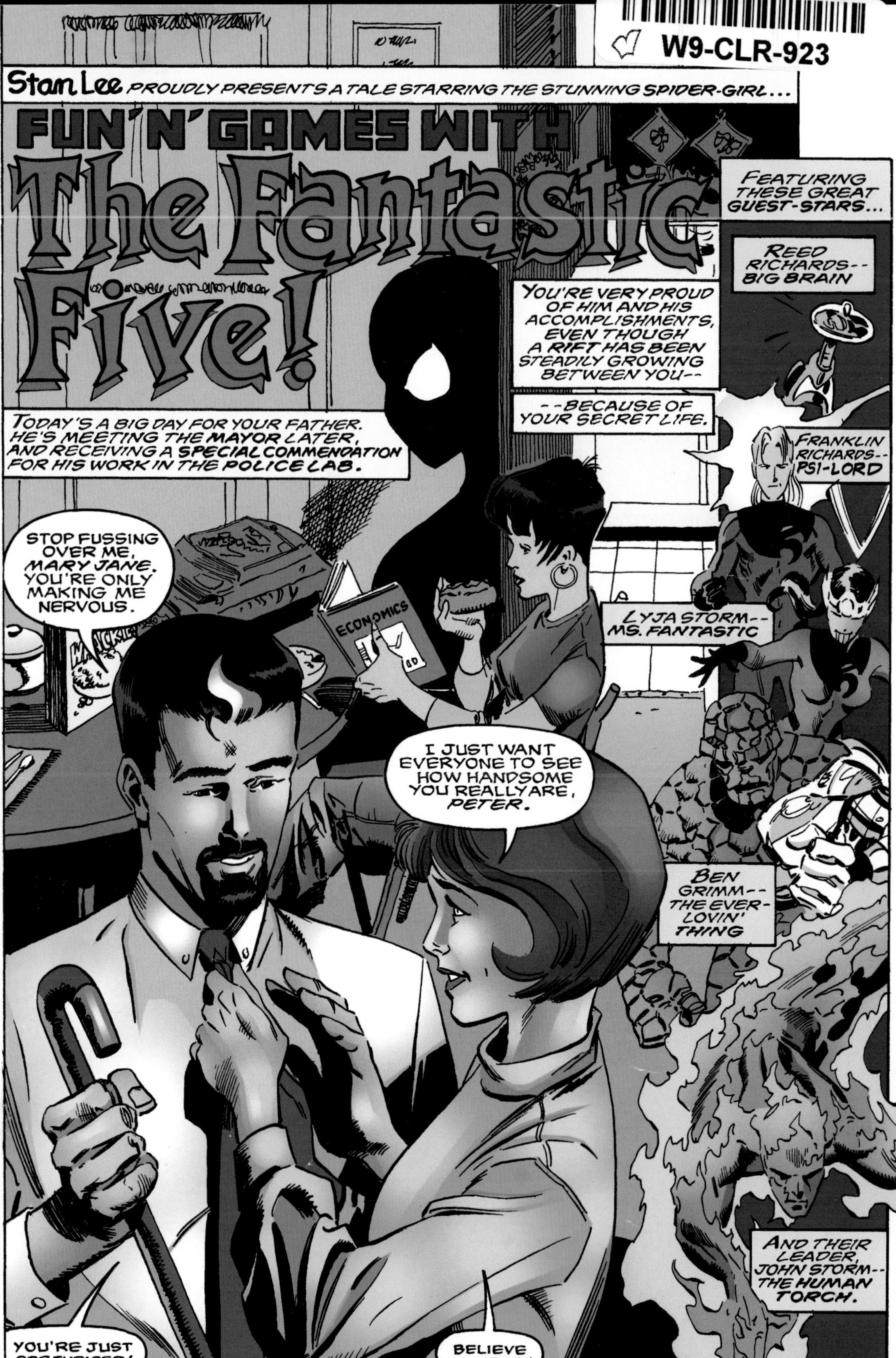
Stan Lee PROUDLY PRESENTS A TALE STARRING THE STUNNING SPIDER-GIRL...
FUN 'N' GAMES WITH
The Fantastic Five!
FEATURING THESE GREAT GUEST-STARS...
REED RICHARDS-- BIG BRAIN
YOU'RE VERY PROUD OF HIM AND HIS ACCOMPLISHMENTS, EVEN THOUGH A RIFT HAS BEEN STEADILY GROWING BETWEEN YOU--
--BECAUSE OF YOUR SECRET LIFE.
TODAY'S A BIG DAY FOR YOUR FATHER. HE'S MEETING THE MAYOR LATER, AND RECEIVING A SPECIAL COMMENDATION FOR HIS WORK IN THE POLICE LAB.
FRANKLIN RICHARDS-- PSI-LORD
STOP FUSSING OVER ME, MARY JANE. YOU'RE ONLY MAKING ME NERVOUS.
ECONOMICS
LYJA STORM-- MS. FANTASTIC
I JUST WANT EVERYONE TO SEE HOW HANDSOME YOU REALLY ARE, PETER.
BEN GRIMM-- THE EVER-LOVIN' THING
AND THEIR LEADER, JOHN STORM-- THE HUMAN TORCH.
YOU'RE JUST PREJUDICED!
BELIEVE IT, TIGER!
TOM DEFALCO WRITER • PAT OLLIFFE PENCILER • AL WILLIAMSON INKER • JANICE CHIANG LETTERING • CHRISTIE SCHEELE COLOR ARTIST • BOB HARRAS SIMPLY FANTASTIC

VISIT US AT
www.abdopub.com

Spotlight, a division of ABDO Publishing Company Inc., is the school and library distributor of the Marvel Entertainment books.

Library bound edition © 2006

Library of Congress Cataloging-in-Publication Data

Fun 'N' Games With the Fantastic Five!

ISBN 1-59961-030-2   (Reinforced Library Bound Edition)

All Spotlight books are reinforced library binding and manufactured in the United States of America

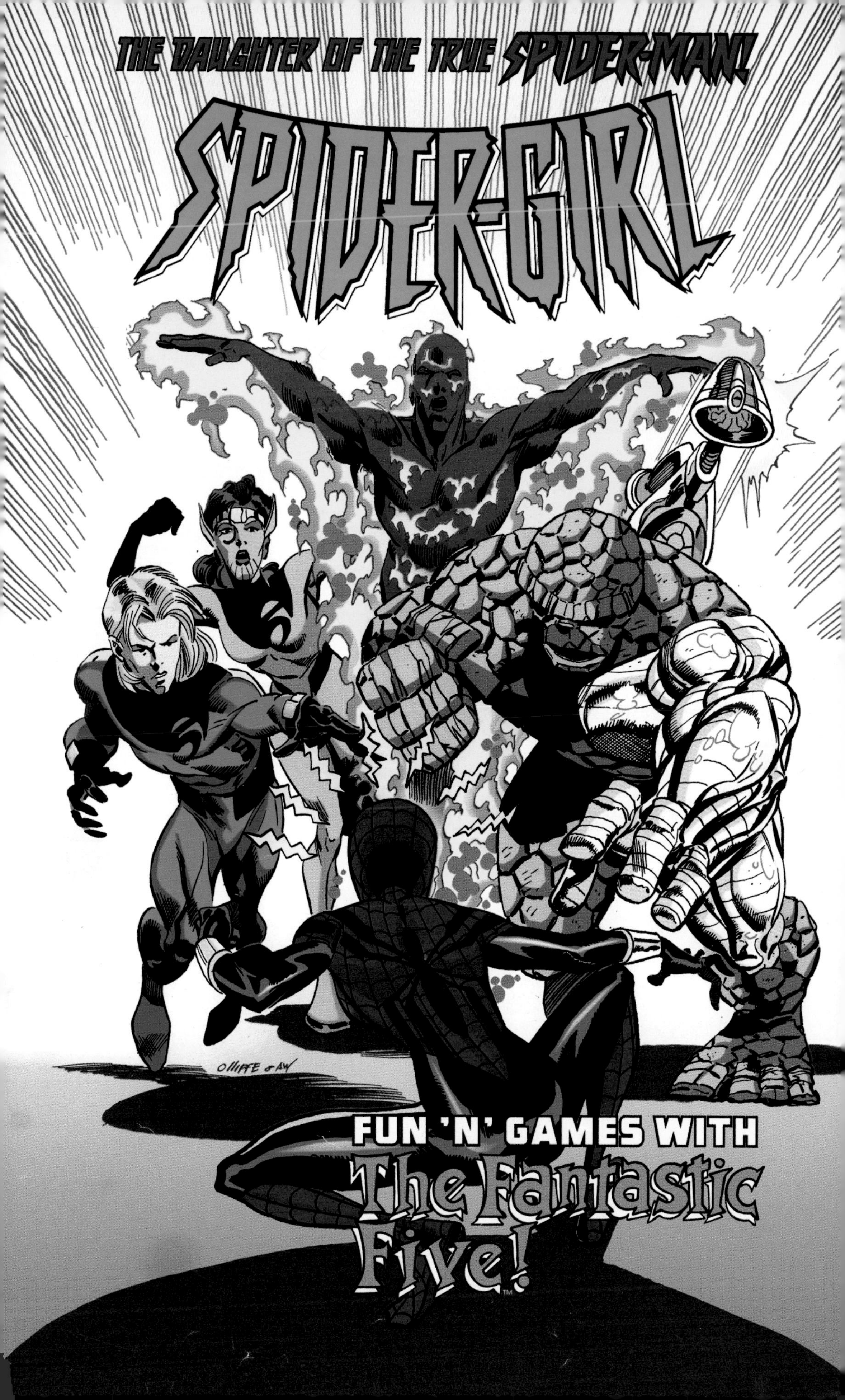
THE DAUGHTER OF THE TRUE SPIDER-MAN!
SPIDER-GIRL
FUN 'N' GAMES WITH
The Fantastic Five!™

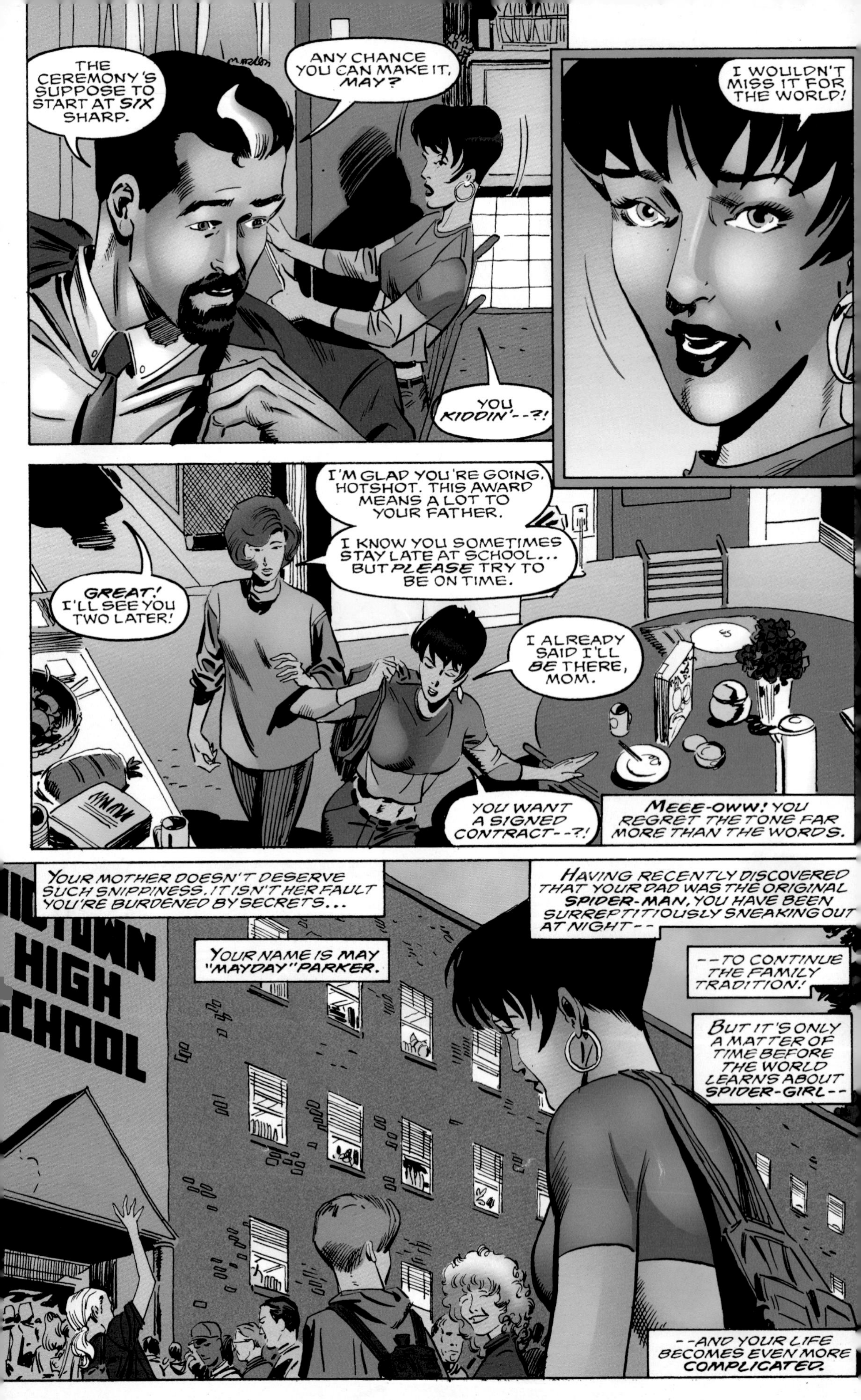

THE CEREMONY'S SUPPOSE TO START AT SIX SHARP.
ANY CHANCE YOU CAN MAKE IT, MAY?
YOU KIDDIN'--?!
I WOULDN'T MISS IT FOR THE WORLD!
I'M GLAD YOU'RE GOING, HOTSHOT. THIS AWARD MEANS A LOT TO YOUR FATHER.
I KNOW YOU SOMETIMES STAY LATE AT SCHOOL... BUT PLEASE TRY TO BE ON TIME.
GREAT! I'LL SEE YOU TWO LATER!
I ALREADY SAID I'LL BE THERE, MOM.
YOU WANT A SIGNED CONTRACT--?!
MEEE-OWW! YOU REGRET THE TONE FAR MORE THAN THE WORDS.
YOUR MOTHER DOESN'T DESERVE SUCH SNIPPINESS. IT ISN'T HER FAULT YOU'RE BURDENED BY SECRETS...
YOUR NAME IS MAY "MAYDAY" PARKER.
HAVING RECENTLY DISCOVERED THAT YOUR DAD WAS THE ORIGINAL SPIDER-MAN, YOU HAVE BEEN SURREPTITIOUSLY SNEAKING OUT AT NIGHT--
--TO CONTINUE THE FAMILY TRADITION!
BUT IT'S ONLY A MATTER OF TIME BEFORE THE WORLD LEARNS ABOUT SPIDER-GIRL--
--AND YOUR LIFE BECOMES EVEN MORE COMPLICATED.
HIGH SCHOOL

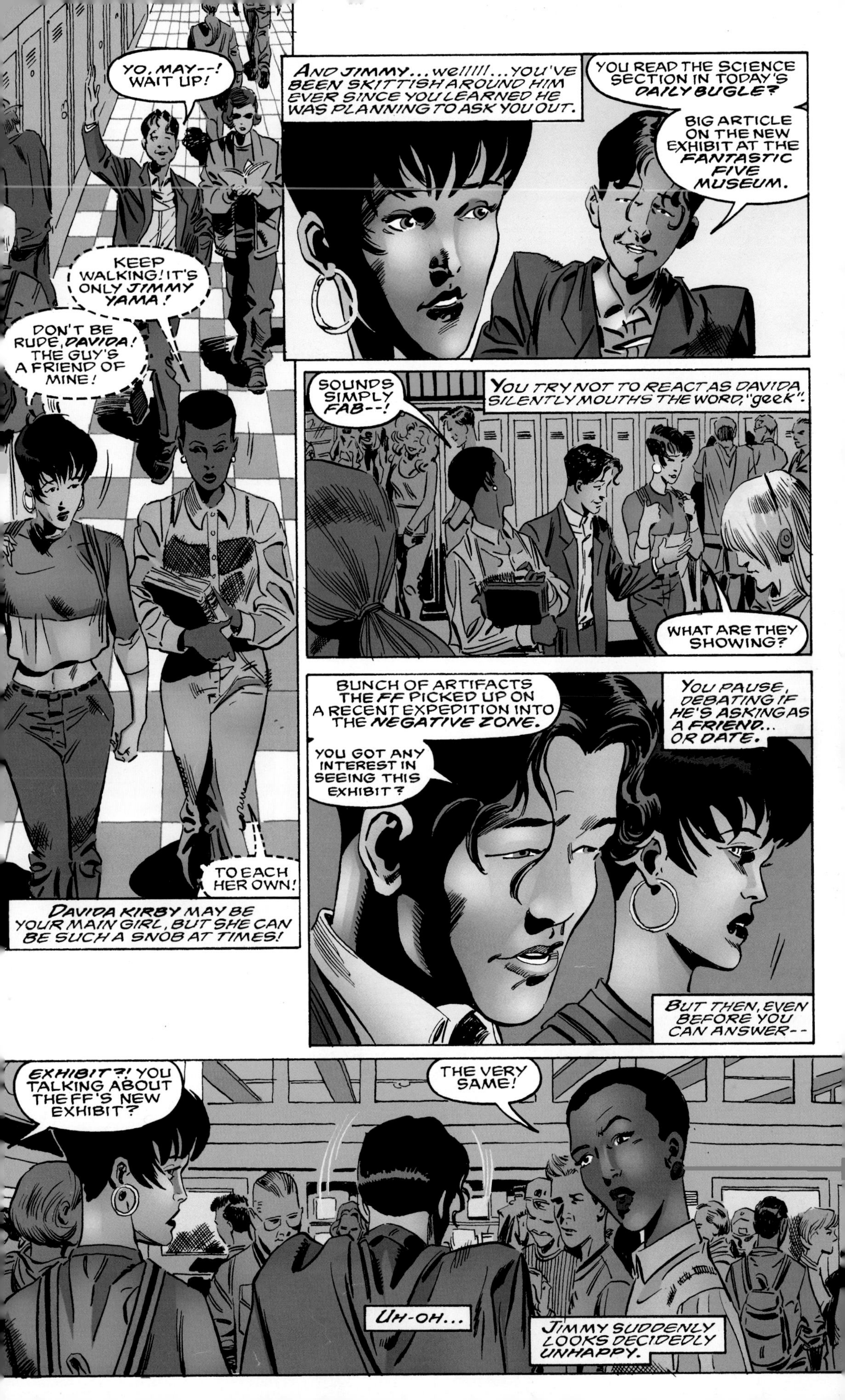
YO, MAY--! WAIT UP!
KEEP WALKING! IT'S ONLY JIMMY YAMA!
DON'T BE RUDE, DAVIDA! THE GUY'S A FRIEND OF MINE!
TO EACH HER OWN!
DAVIDA KIRBY MAY BE YOUR MAIN GIRL, BUT SHE CAN BE SUCH A SNOB AT TIMES!
AND JIMMY... wellll... YOU'VE BEEN SKITTISH AROUND HIM EVER SINCE YOU LEARNED HE WAS PLANNING TO ASK YOU OUT.
YOU READ THE SCIENCE SECTION IN TODAY'S DAILY BUGLE?
BIG ARTICLE ON THE NEW EXHIBIT AT THE FANTASTIC FIVE MUSEUM.
SOUNDS SIMPLY FAB--!
YOU TRY NOT TO REACT AS DAVIDA SILENTLY MOUTHS THE WORD, "geek".
WHAT ARE THEY SHOWING?
BUNCH OF ARTIFACTS THE FF PICKED UP ON A RECENT EXPEDITION INTO THE NEGATIVE ZONE.
YOU GOT ANY INTEREST IN SEEING THIS EXHIBIT?
YOU PAUSE, DEBATING IF HE'S ASKING AS A FRIEND... OR DATE.
BUT THEN, EVEN BEFORE YOU CAN ANSWER--
EXHIBIT?! YOU TALKING ABOUT THE FF'S NEW EXHIBIT?
THE VERY SAME!
UH-OH...
JIMMY SUDDENLY LOOKS DECIDEDLY UNHAPPY.

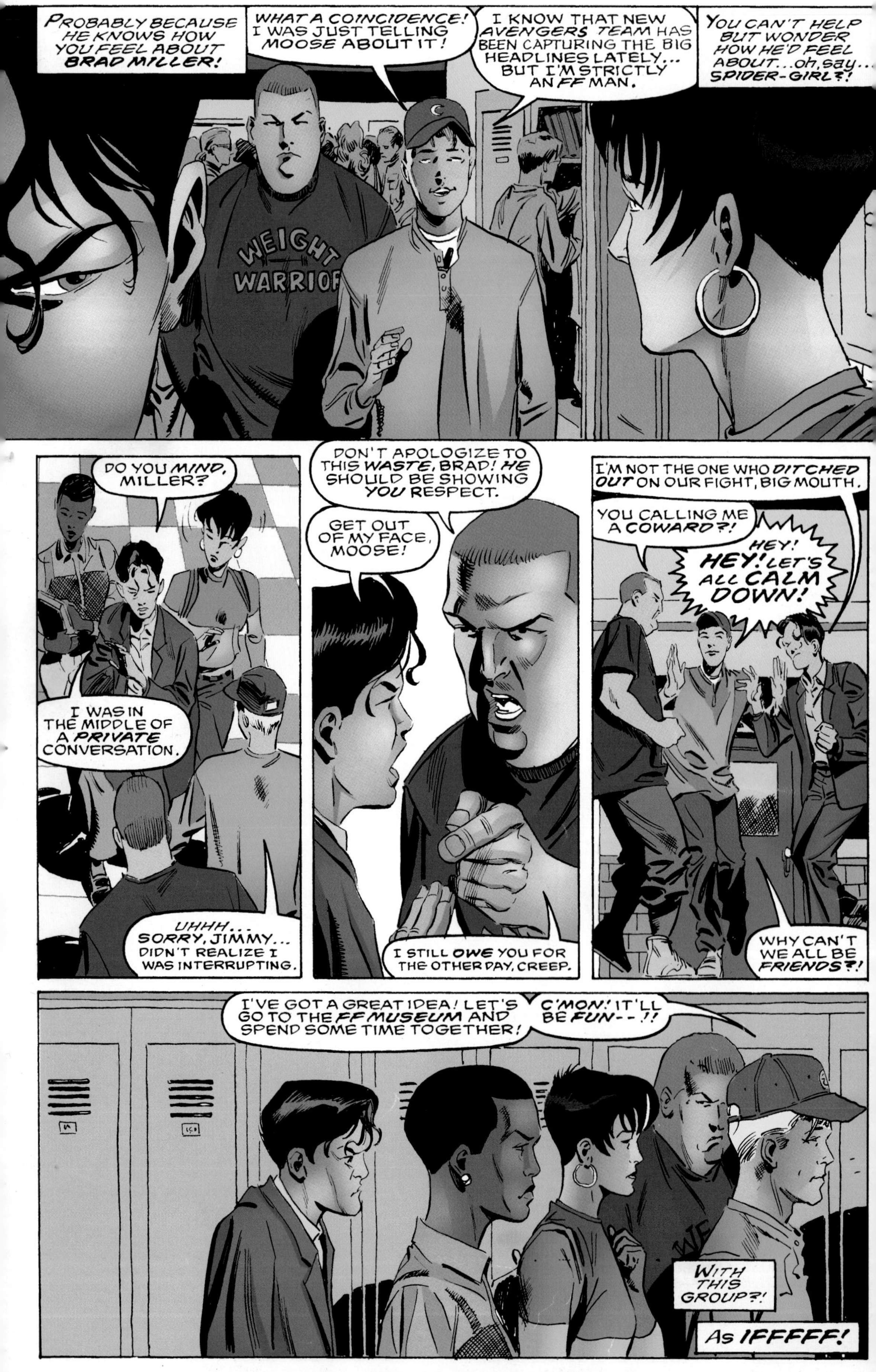
PROBABLY BECAUSE HE KNOWS HOW YOU FEEL ABOUT BRAD MILLER!
WHAT A COINCIDENCE! I WAS JUST TELLING MOOSE ABOUT IT!
I KNOW THAT NEW AVENGERS TEAM HAS BEEN CAPTURING THE BIG HEADLINES LATELY... BUT I'M STRICTLY AN FF MAN.
YOU CAN'T HELP BUT WONDER HOW HE'D FEEL ABOUT...oh, say... SPIDER-GIRL?!
WEIGHT WARRIOR
DO YOU MIND, MILLER?
I WAS IN THE MIDDLE OF A PRIVATE CONVERSATION.
UHHH... SORRY, JIMMY... DIDN'T REALIZE I WAS INTERRUPTING.
DON'T APOLOGIZE TO THIS WASTE, BRAD! HE SHOULD BE SHOWING YOU RESPECT.
GET OUT OF MY FACE, MOOSE!
I STILL OWE YOU FOR THE OTHER DAY, CREEP.
I'M NOT THE ONE WHO DITCHED OUT ON OUR FIGHT, BIG MOUTH.
YOU CALLING ME A COWARD?!
HEY! HEY! LET'S ALL CALM DOWN!
WHY CAN'T WE ALL BE FRIENDS?!
I'VE GOT A GREAT IDEA! LET'S GO TO THE FF MUSEUM AND SPEND SOME TIME TOGETHER!
C'MON! IT'LL BE FUN--!!
WITH THIS GROUP?!
As IFFFFF!

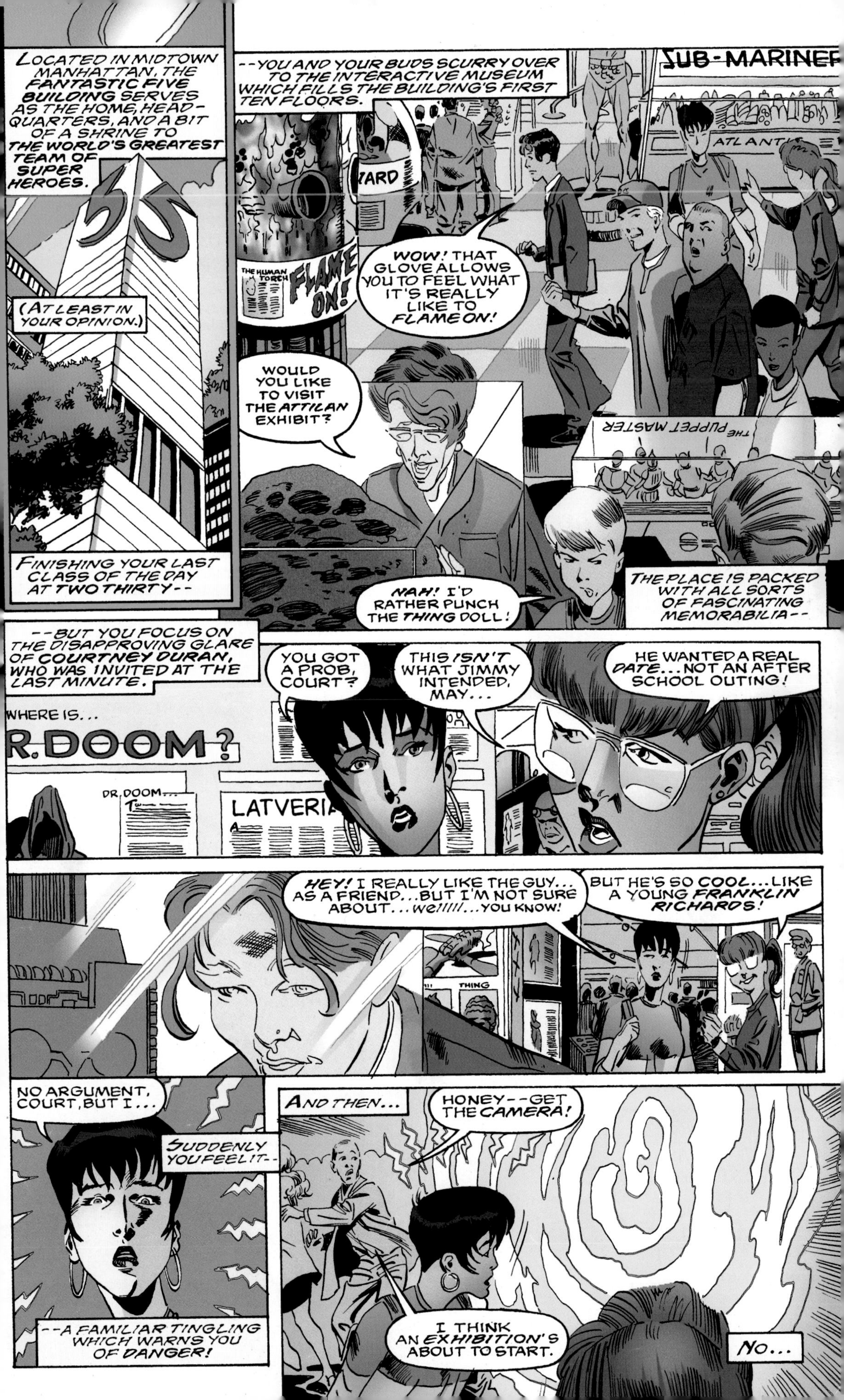
LOCATED IN MIDTOWN MANHATTAN, THE FANTASTIC FIVE BUILDING SERVES AS THE HOME, HEAD-QUARTERS, AND A BIT OF A SHRINE TO THE WORLD'S GREATEST TEAM OF SUPER HEROES.
(AT LEAST IN YOUR OPINION.)
FINISHING YOUR LAST CLASS OF THE DAY AT TWO THIRTY--
--YOU AND YOUR BUDS SCURRY OVER TO THE INTERACTIVE MUSEUM WHICH FILLS THE BUILDING'S FIRST TEN FLOORS.
SUB-MARINER
THE HUMAN TORCH
FLAME ON!
WOW! THAT GLOVE ALLOWS YOU TO FEEL WHAT IT'S REALLY LIKE TO FLAME ON!
WOULD YOU LIKE TO VISIT THE ATTILAN EXHIBIT?
THE PUPPET MASTER
NAH! I'D RATHER PUNCH THE THING DOLL!
THE PLACE IS PACKED WITH ALL SORTS OF FASCINATING MEMORABILIA--
--BUT YOU FOCUS ON THE DISAPPROVING GLARE OF COURTNEY DURAN, WHO WAS INVITED AT THE LAST MINUTE.
YOU GOT A PROB, COURT?
THIS ISN'T WHAT JIMMY INTENDED, MAY...
HE WANTED A REAL DATE... NOT AN AFTER SCHOOL OUTING!
WHERE IS...
R. DOOM?
DR. DOOM...
LATVERIA
HEY! I REALLY LIKE THE GUY... AS A FRIEND... BUT I'M NOT SURE ABOUT... wellll... YOU KNOW!
BUT HE'S SO COOL... LIKE A YOUNG FRANKLIN RICHARDS!
THING
NO ARGUMENT, COURT, BUT I...
SUDDENLY YOU FEEL IT--
--A FAMILIAR TINGLING WHICH WARNS YOU OF DANGER!
AND THEN...
HONEY--GET THE CAMERA!
I THINK AN EXHIBITION'S ABOUT TO START.
NO...

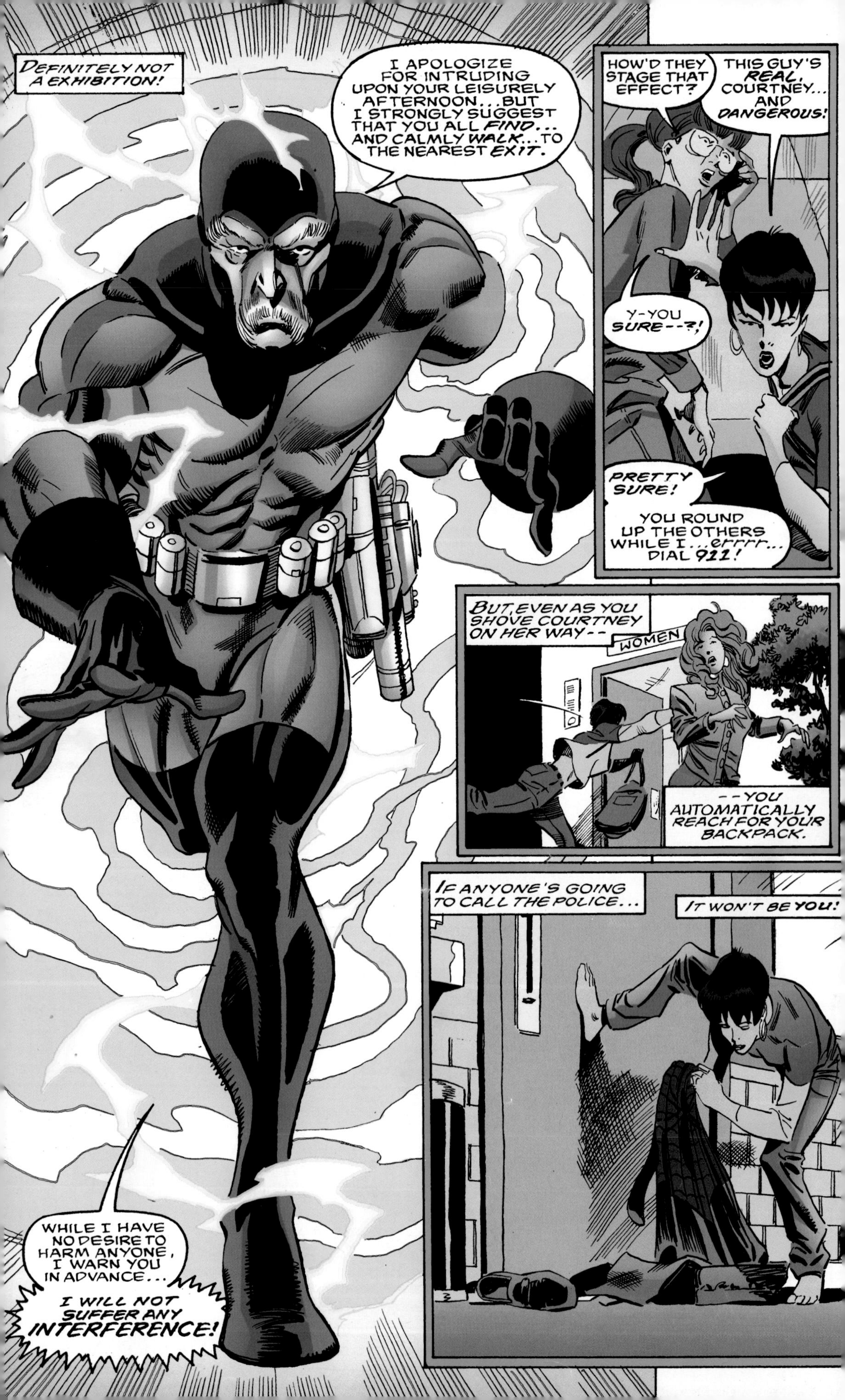
DEFINITELY NOT A EXHIBITION!
I APOLOGIZE FOR INTRUDING UPON YOUR LEISURELY AFTERNOON...BUT I STRONGLY SUGGEST THAT YOU ALL FIND... AND CALMLY WALK...TO THE NEAREST EXIT.
WHILE I HAVE NO DESIRE TO HARM ANYONE, I WARN YOU IN ADVANCE...
I WILL NOT SUFFER ANY INTERFERENCE!
HOW'D THEY STAGE THAT EFFECT?
THIS GUY'S REAL, COURTNEY... AND DANGEROUS!
Y-YOU SURE--?!
PRETTY SURE!
YOU ROUND UP THE OTHERS WHILE I...errrr... DIAL 911!
BUT, EVEN AS YOU SHOVE COURTNEY ON HER WAY--
WOMEN
--YOU AUTOMATICALLY REACH FOR YOUR BACKPACK.
IF ANYONE'S GOING TO CALL THE POLICE...
IT WON'T BE YOU!

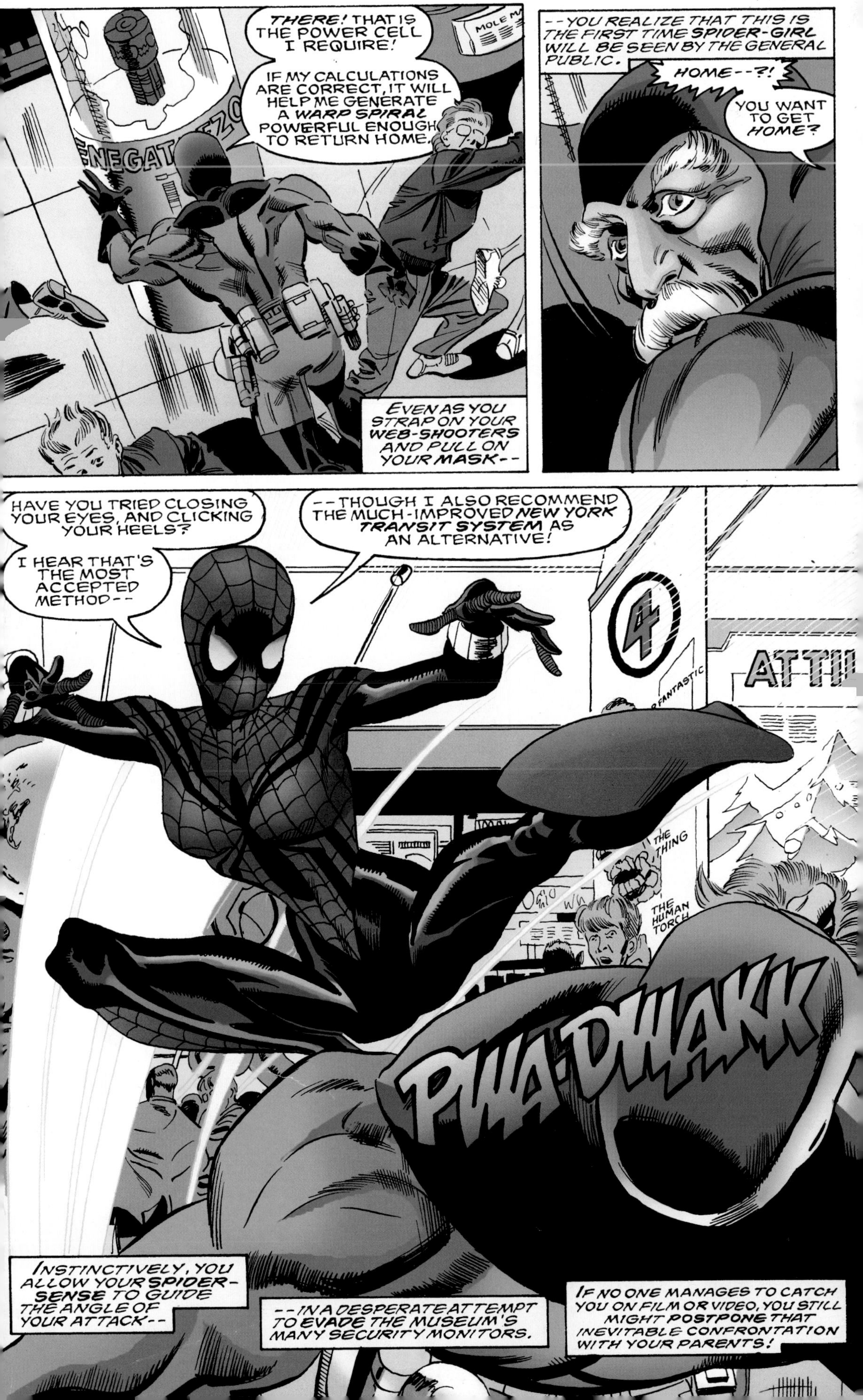

THERE! THAT IS THE POWER CELL I REQUIRE!
IF MY CALCULATIONS ARE CORRECT, IT WILL HELP ME GENERATE A WARP SPIRAL POWERFUL ENOUGH TO RETURN HOME.
EVEN AS YOU STRAP ON YOUR WEB-SHOOTERS AND PULL ON YOUR MASK--
--YOU REALIZE THAT THIS IS THE FIRST TIME SPIDER-GIRL WILL BE SEEN BY THE GENERAL PUBLIC.
HOME--?!
YOU WANT TO GET HOME?
HAVE YOU TRIED CLOSING YOUR EYES, AND CLICKING YOUR HEELS?
I HEAR THAT'S THE MOST ACCEPTED METHOD--
--THOUGH I ALSO RECOMMEND THE MUCH-IMPROVED NEW YORK TRANSIT SYSTEM AS AN ALTERNATIVE!
THE THING
THE HUMAN TORCH
PWA-DWAKK
INSTINCTIVELY, YOU ALLOW YOUR SPIDER-SENSE TO GUIDE THE ANGLE OF YOUR ATTACK--
--IN A DESPERATE ATTEMPT TO EVADE THE MUSEUM'S MANY SECURITY MONITORS.
IF NO ONE MANAGES TO CATCH YOU ON FILM OR VIDEO, YOU STILL MIGHT POSTPONE THAT INEVITABLE CONFRONTATION WITH YOUR PARENTS!

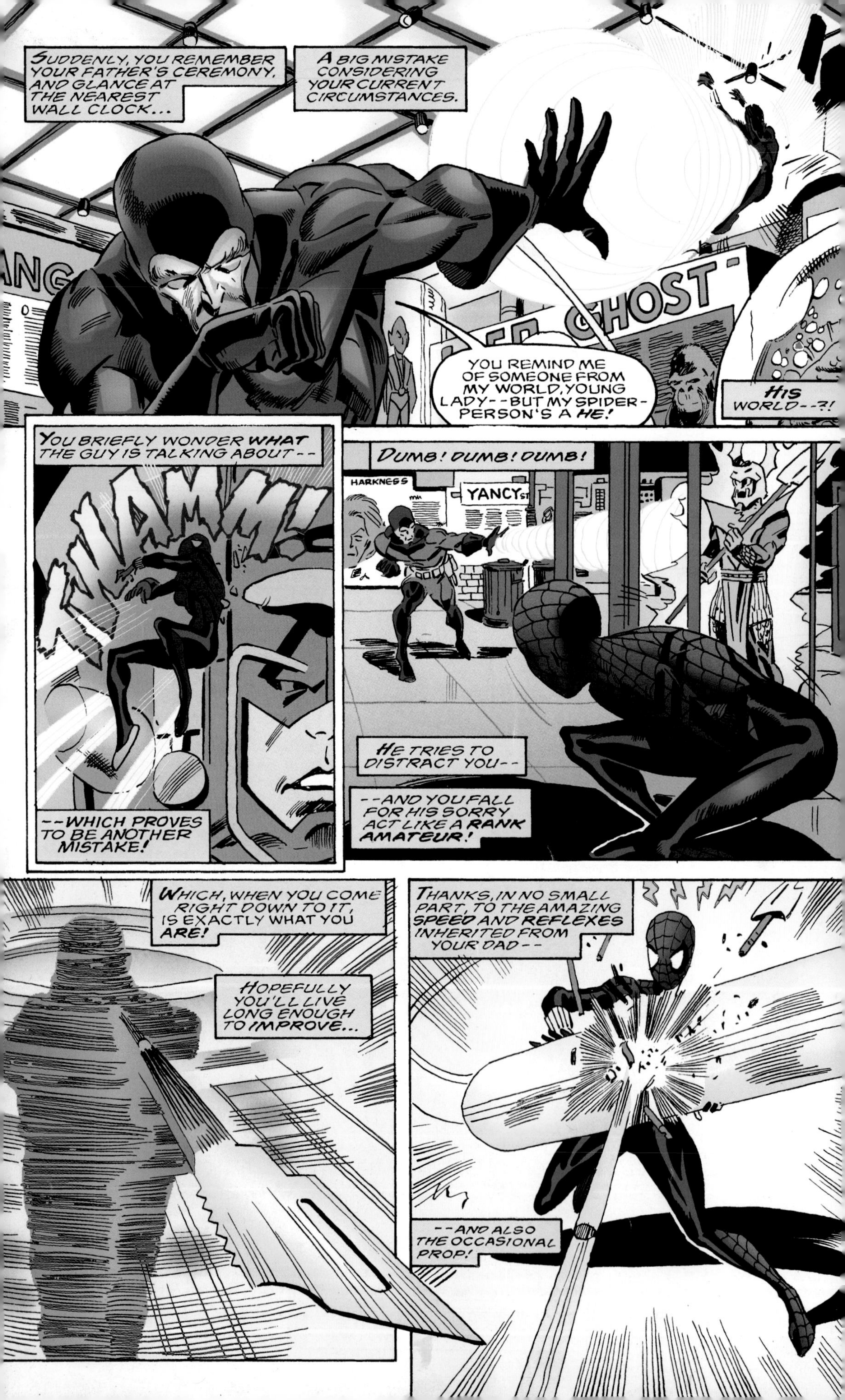

SUDDENLY, YOU REMEMBER YOUR FATHER'S CEREMONY, AND GLANCE AT THE NEAREST WALL CLOCK...
A BIG MISTAKE CONSIDERING YOUR CURRENT CIRCUMSTANCES.
YOU REMIND ME OF SOMEONE FROM MY WORLD, YOUNG LADY--BUT MY SPIDER-PERSON'S A HE!
HIS WORLD--?!
YOU BRIEFLY WONDER WHAT THE GUY IS TALKING ABOUT--
--WHICH PROVES TO BE ANOTHER MISTAKE!
DUMB! DUMB! DUMB!
HARKNESS
YANCY ST
HE TRIES TO DISTRACT YOU--
--AND YOU FALL FOR HIS SORRY ACT LIKE A RANK AMATEUR!
WHICH, WHEN YOU COME RIGHT DOWN TO IT, IS EXACTLY WHAT YOU ARE!
HOPEFULLY YOU'LL LIVE LONG ENOUGH TO IMPROVE...
THANKS, IN NO SMALL PART, TO THE AMAZING SPEED AND REFLEXES INHERITED FROM YOUR DAD--
--AND ALSO THE OCCASIONAL PROP!

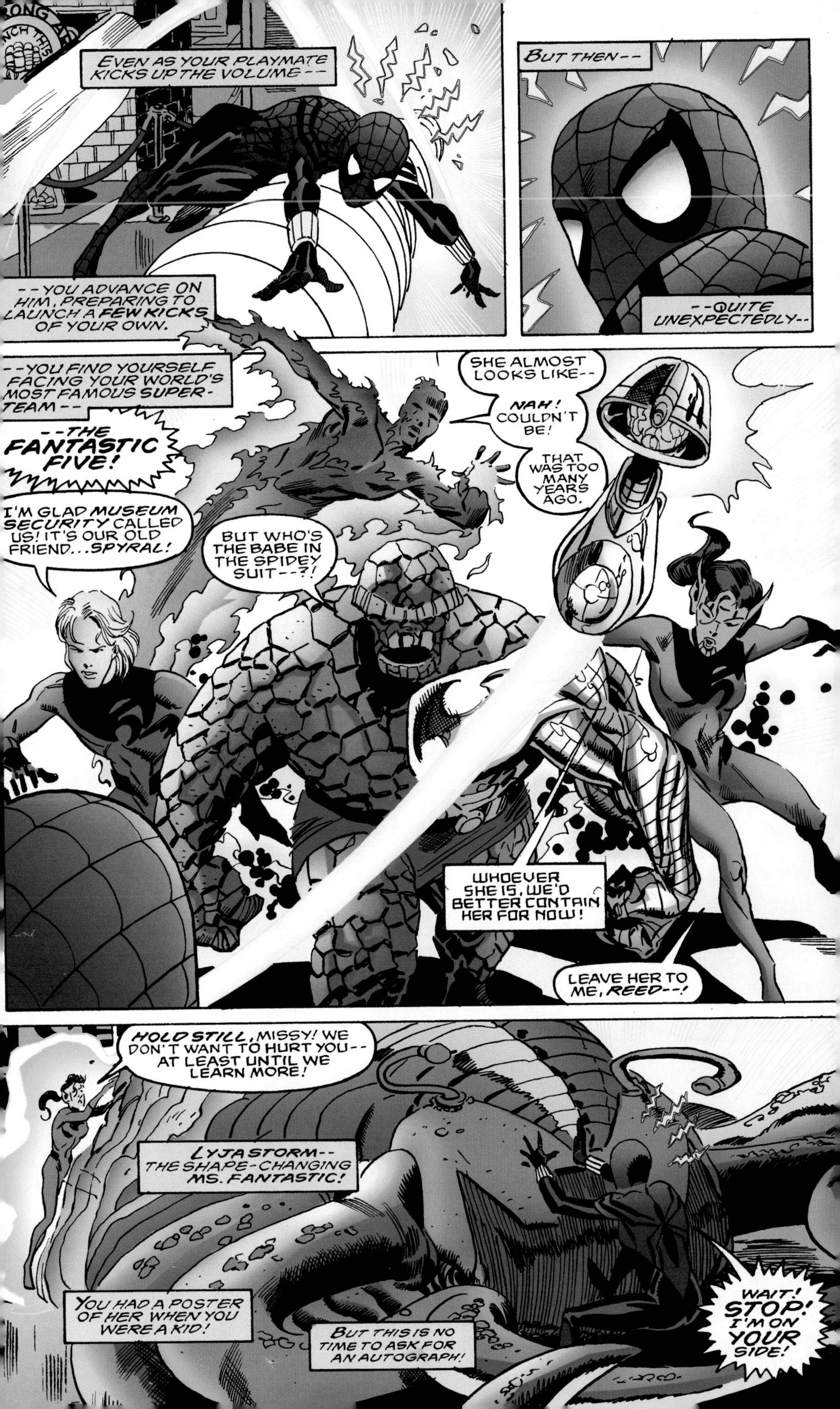
EVEN AS YOUR PLAYMATE KICKS UP THE VOLUME--
--YOU ADVANCE ON HIM, PREPARING TO LAUNCH A FEW KICKS OF YOUR OWN.
BUT THEN--
--QUITE UNEXPECTEDLY--
--YOU FIND YOURSELF FACING YOUR WORLD'S MOST FAMOUS SUPER-TEAM--
--THE FANTASTIC FIVE!
SHE ALMOST LOOKS LIKE--
NAH! COULDN'T BE!
THAT WAS TOO MANY YEARS AGO.
I'M GLAD MUSEUM SECURITY CALLED US! IT'S OUR OLD FRIEND...SPYRAL!
BUT WHO'S THE BABE IN THE SPIDEY SUIT--?!
WHOEVER SHE IS, WE'D BETTER CONTAIN HER FOR NOW!
LEAVE HER TO ME, REED--!
HOLD STILL, MISSY! WE DON'T WANT TO HURT YOU--AT LEAST UNTIL WE LEARN MORE!
LYJA STORM--THE SHAPE-CHANGING MS. FANTASTIC!
YOU HAD A POSTER OF HER WHEN YOU WERE A KID!
BUT THIS IS NO TIME TO ASK FOR AN AUTOGRAPH!
WAIT! STOP! I'M ON YOUR SIDE!

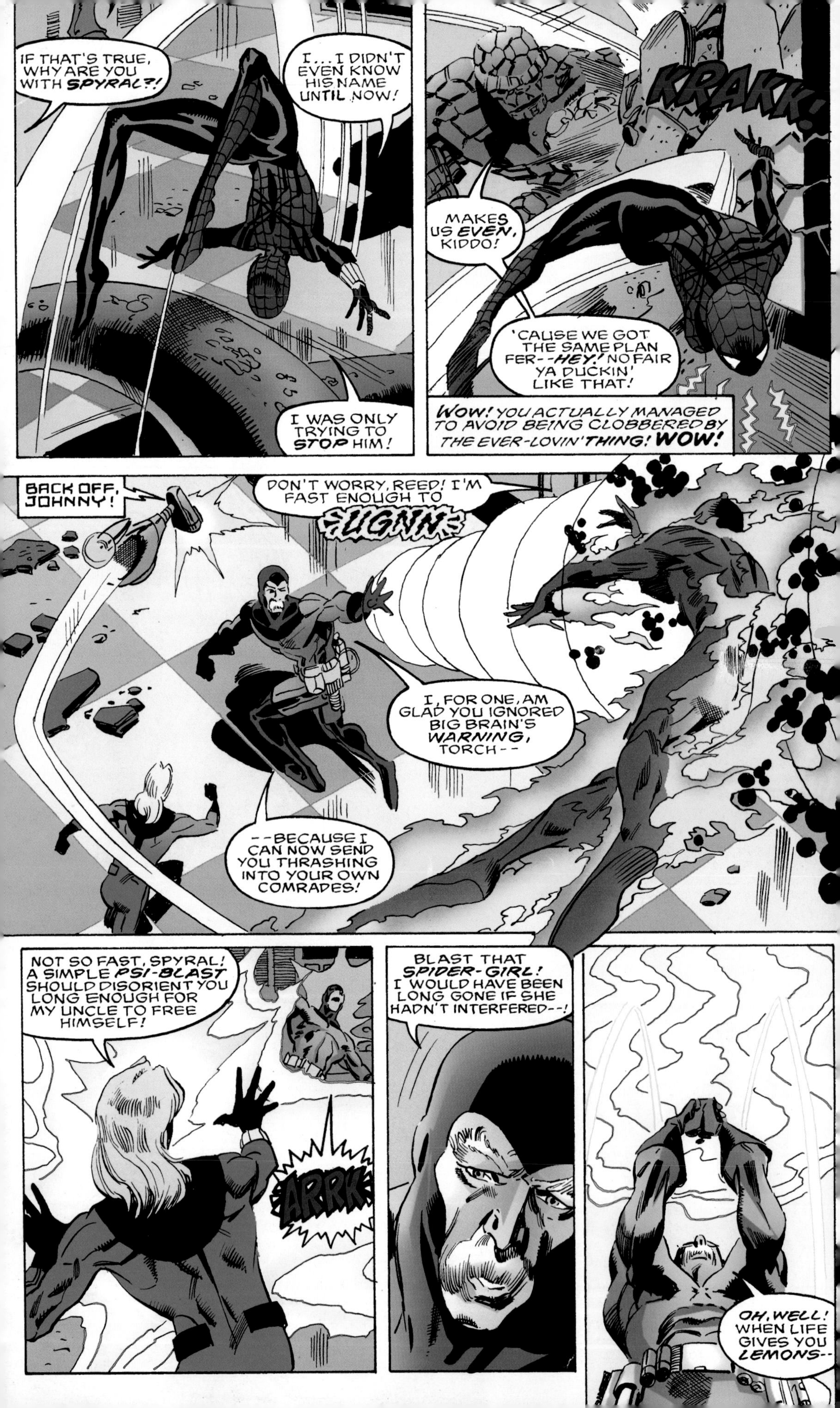
IF THAT'S TRUE, WHY ARE YOU WITH SPYRAL?!
I... I DIDN'T EVEN KNOW HIS NAME UNTIL NOW!
I WAS ONLY TRYING TO STOP HIM!
KRAKK!
MAKES US EVEN, KIDDO!
'CAUSE WE GOT THE SAME PLAN FER--HEY! NO FAIR YA DUCKIN' LIKE THAT!
WOW! YOU ACTUALLY MANAGED TO AVOID BEING CLOBBERED BY THE EVER-LOVIN' THING! WOW!
BACK OFF, JOHNNY!
DON'T WORRY, REED! I'M FAST ENOUGH TO
UGNN
I, FOR ONE, AM GLAD YOU IGNORED BIG BRAIN'S WARNING, TORCH--
--BECAUSE I CAN NOW SEND YOU THRASHING INTO YOUR OWN COMRADES!
NOT SO FAST, SPYRAL! A SIMPLE PSI-BLAST SHOULD DISORIENT YOU LONG ENOUGH FOR MY UNCLE TO FREE HIMSELF!
ARRK
BLAST THAT SPIDER-GIRL! I WOULD HAVE BEEN LONG GONE IF SHE HADN'T INTERFERED--!
OH, WELL! WHEN LIFE GIVES YOU LEMONS--

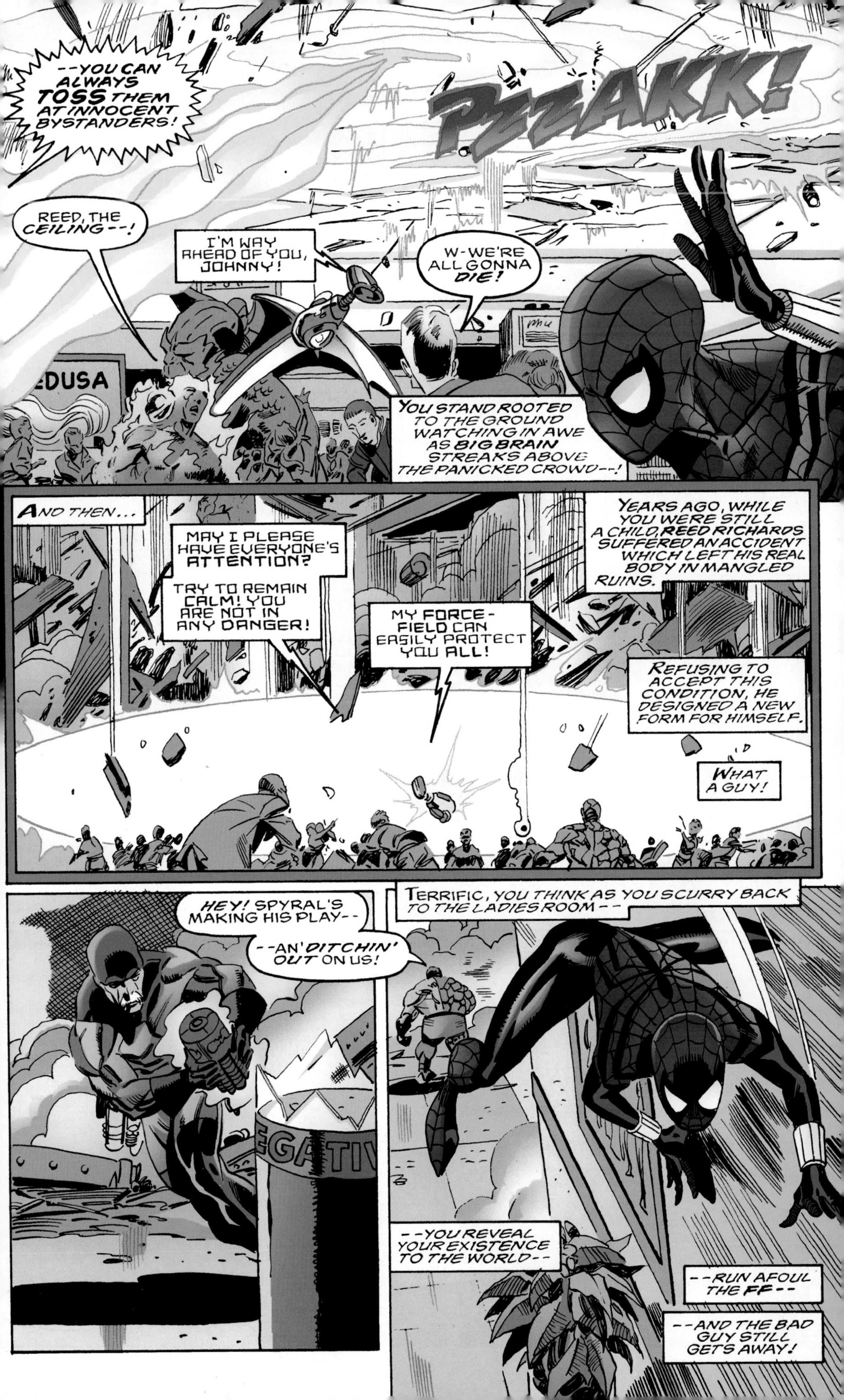
--YOU CAN ALWAYS TOSS THEM AT INNOCENT BYSTANDERS!
PZZAKK!
REED, THE CEILING--!
I'M WAY AHEAD OF YOU, JOHNNY!
W-WE'RE ALL GONNA DIE!
EDUSA
YOU STAND ROOTED TO THE GROUND WATCHING IN AWE AS BIG BRAIN STREAKS ABOVE THE PANICKED CROWD--!
AND THEN...
MAY I PLEASE HAVE EVERYONE'S ATTENTION?
TRY TO REMAIN CALM! YOU ARE NOT IN ANY DANGER!
MY FORCE-FIELD CAN EASILY PROTECT YOU ALL!
YEARS AGO, WHILE YOU WERE STILL A CHILD, REED RICHARDS SUFFERED AN ACCIDENT WHICH LEFT HIS REAL BODY IN MANGLED RUINS.
REFUSING TO ACCEPT THIS CONDITION, HE DESIGNED A NEW FORM FOR HIMSELF.
WHAT A GUY!
HEY! SPYRAL'S MAKING HIS PLAY--
--AN' DITCHIN' OUT ON US!
TERRIFIC, YOU THINK AS YOU SCURRY BACK TO THE LADIES ROOM--
EGATIV
--YOU REVEAL YOUR EXISTENCE TO THE WORLD--
--RUN AFOUL THE FF--
--AND THE BAD GUY STILL GETS AWAY!

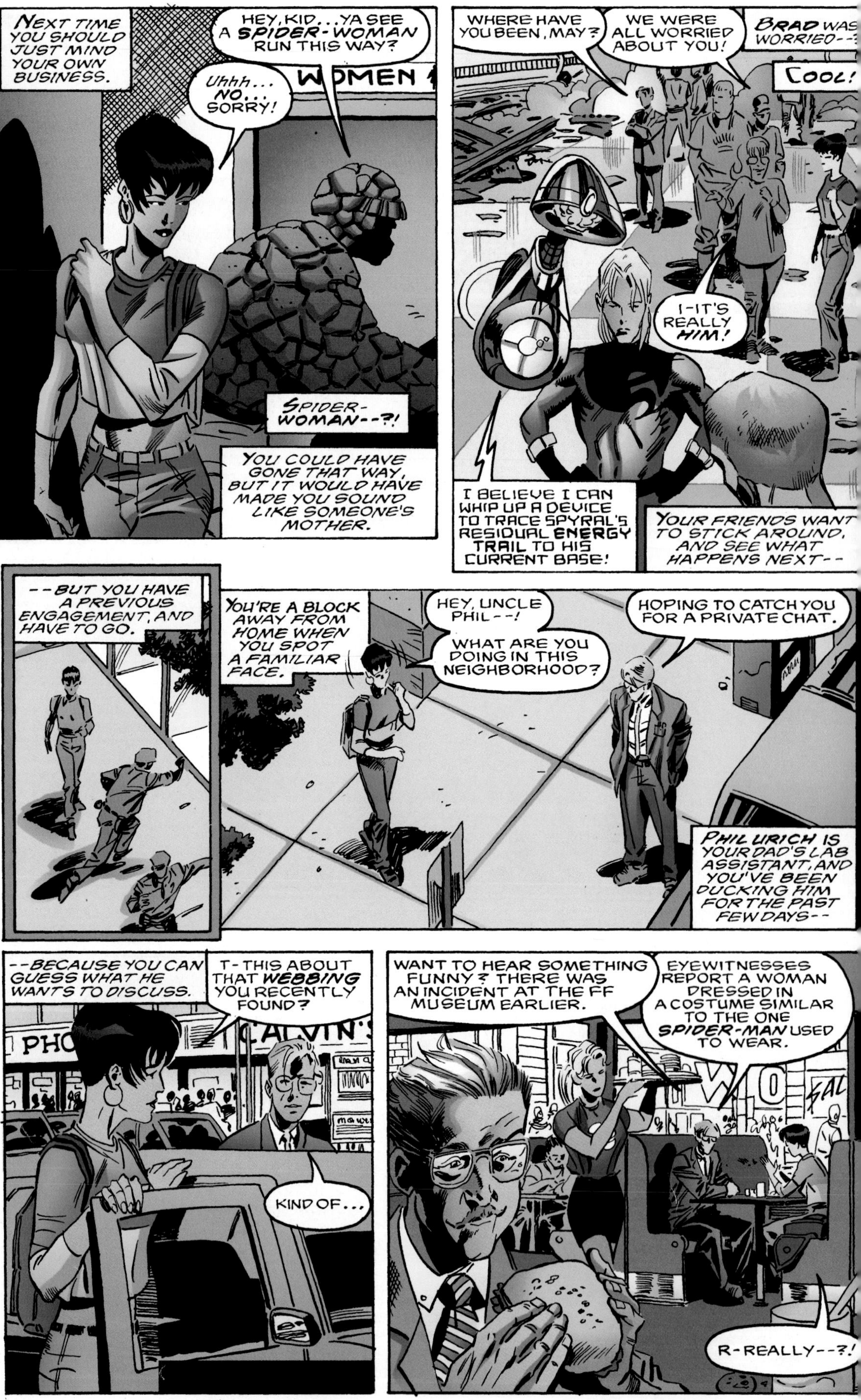
NEXT TIME YOU SHOULD JUST MIND YOUR OWN BUSINESS.
HEY, KID...YA SEE A SPIDER-WOMAN RUN THIS WAY?
Uhhh... NO... SORRY!
WOMEN
SPIDER-WOMAN--?!
YOU COULD HAVE GONE THAT WAY, BUT IT WOULD HAVE MADE YOU SOUND LIKE SOMEONE'S MOTHER.
WHERE HAVE YOU BEEN, MAY?
WE WERE ALL WORRIED ABOUT YOU!
BRAD WAS WORRIED--
COOL!
I-IT'S REALLY HIM!
I BELIEVE I CAN WHIP UP A DEVICE TO TRACE SPYRAL'S RESIDUAL ENERGY TRAIL TO HIS CURRENT BASE!
YOUR FRIENDS WANT TO STICK AROUND, AND SEE WHAT HAPPENS NEXT--
--BUT YOU HAVE A PREVIOUS ENGAGEMENT, AND HAVE TO GO.
YOU'RE A BLOCK AWAY FROM HOME WHEN YOU SPOT A FAMILIAR FACE.
HEY, UNCLE PHIL--!
WHAT ARE YOU DOING IN THIS NEIGHBORHOOD?
HOPING TO CATCH YOU FOR A PRIVATE CHAT.
PHIL URICH IS YOUR DAD'S LAB ASSISTANT, AND YOU'VE BEEN DUCKING HIM FOR THE PAST FEW DAYS--
--BECAUSE YOU CAN GUESS WHAT HE WANTS TO DISCUSS.
T-THIS ABOUT THAT WEBBING YOU RECENTLY FOUND?
KIND OF...
WANT TO HEAR SOMETHING FUNNY? THERE WAS AN INCIDENT AT THE FF MUSEUM EARLIER.
EYEWITNESSES REPORT A WOMAN DRESSED IN A COSTUME SIMILAR TO THE ONE SPIDER-MAN USED TO WEAR.
R-REALLY--?!

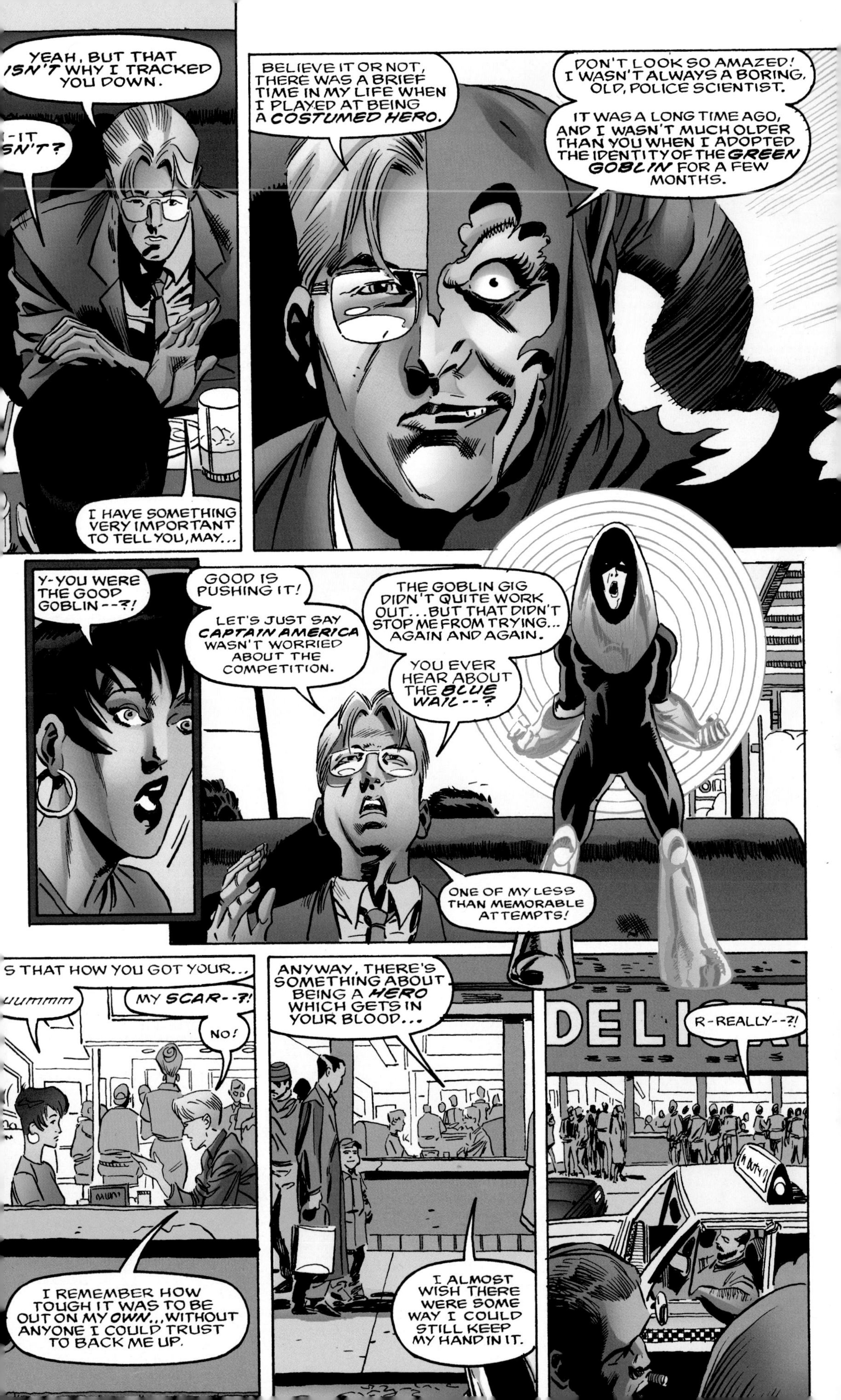
YEAH, BUT THAT ISN'T WHY I TRACKED YOU DOWN.
I-IT ISN'T?
I HAVE SOMETHING VERY IMPORTANT TO TELL YOU, MAY...
BELIEVE IT OR NOT, THERE WAS A BRIEF TIME IN MY LIFE WHEN I PLAYED AT BEING A COSTUMED HERO.
DON'T LOOK SO AMAZED! I WASN'T ALWAYS A BORING, OLD, POLICE SCIENTIST.
IT WAS A LONG TIME AGO, AND I WASN'T MUCH OLDER THAN YOU WHEN I ADOPTED THE IDENTITY OF THE GREEN GOBLIN FOR A FEW MONTHS.
Y-YOU WERE THE GOOD GOBLIN--?!
GOOD IS PUSHING IT!
LET'S JUST SAY CAPTAIN AMERICA WASN'T WORRIED ABOUT THE COMPETITION.
THE GOBLIN GIG DIDN'T QUITE WORK OUT...BUT THAT DIDN'T STOP ME FROM TRYING... AGAIN AND AGAIN.
YOU EVER HEAR ABOUT THE BLUE WAIL--?
ONE OF MY LESS THAN MEMORABLE ATTEMPTS!
S THAT HOW YOU GOT YOUR...
UUMMMM
MY SCAR--?!
NO!
I REMEMBER HOW TOUGH IT WAS TO BE OUT ON MY OWN...WITHOUT ANYONE I COULD TRUST TO BACK ME UP.
ANYWAY, THERE'S SOMETHING ABOUT BEING A HERO WHICH GETS IN YOUR BLOOD...
I ALMOST WISH THERE WERE SOME WAY I COULD STILL KEEP MY HAND IN IT.
DELI
R-REALLY--?!

"THERE'S SOMETHING ABOUT BEING A *HERO* WHICH GETS IN YOUR BLOOD."

SURE IS...

OTHERWISE YOU WOULDN'T HAVE DOUBLED BACK TO *FF HEADQUARTERS* TO SEE IF *BIG BRAIN* SUCCEEDED IN WHIPPIN' UP HIS TRACKING GIZMO...

AS THE CLOCK INCHES PAST FIVE, YOU GRUDGINGLY REALIZE IT'S TIME TO HEAD FOR YOUR *DAD'S* AWARD CEREMONY...

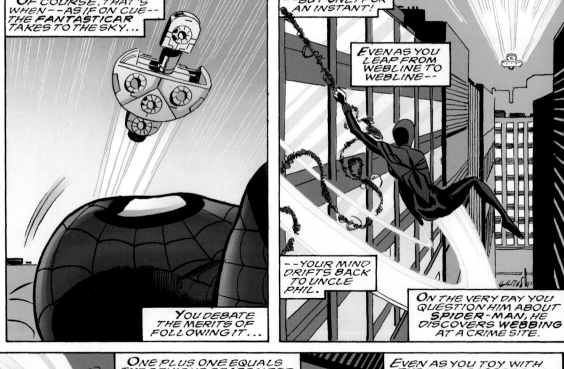

OF COURSE, THAT'S WHEN -- AS IF ON CUE -- THE *FANTASTICAR* TAKES TO THE SKY...

YOU DEBATE THE MERITS OF FOLLOWING IT...

--BUT ONLY FOR AN *INSTANT!*

EVEN AS YOU LEAP FROM WEBLINE TO WEBLINE--

--YOUR MIND DRIFTS BACK TO UNCLE *PHIL.*

ON THE VERY DAY YOU QUESTION HIM ABOUT *SPIDER-MAN,* HE DISCOVERS *WEBBING* AT A CRIME SITE.

ONE PLUS ONE EQUALS THE OBVIOUS REASON FOR TODAY'S REVELATION.

EVEN AS YOU TOY WITH THE IDEA OF ACCEPTING HIS NOT SO VEILED OFFER, THE *FF* VEER TOWARD *STANDARD VILLAIN HIDEOUT #3...*

...THE SEEMINGLY DESERTED WAREHOUSE.

317

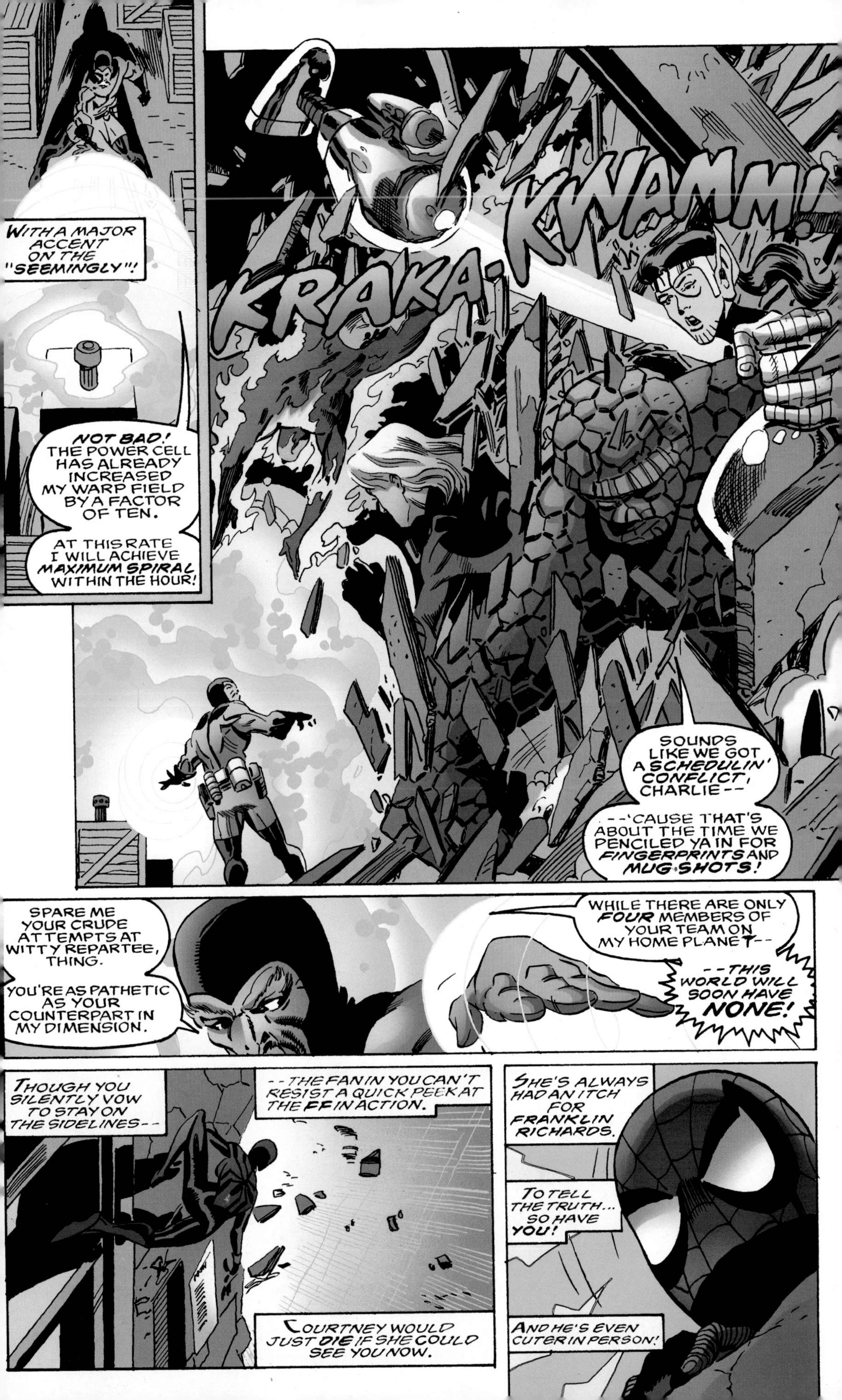
WITH A MAJOR ACCENT ON THE "SEEMINGLY"!
KRAKA-KWAMM!
NOT BAD! THE POWER CELL HAS ALREADY INCREASED MY WARP FIELD BY A FACTOR OF TEN.
AT THIS RATE I WILL ACHIEVE MAXIMUM SPIRAL WITHIN THE HOUR!
SOUNDS LIKE WE GOT A SCHEDULIN' CONFLICT, CHARLIE--
--'CAUSE THAT'S ABOUT THE TIME WE PENCILED YA IN FOR FINGERPRINTS AND MUG SHOTS!
SPARE ME YOUR CRUDE ATTEMPTS AT WITTY REPARTEE, THING.
YOU'RE AS PATHETIC AS YOUR COUNTERPART IN MY DIMENSION.
WHILE THERE ARE ONLY FOUR MEMBERS OF YOUR TEAM ON MY HOME PLANET--
--THIS WORLD WILL SOON HAVE NONE!
THOUGH YOU SILENTLY VOW TO STAY ON THE SIDELINES--
--THE FAN IN YOU CAN'T RESIST A QUICK PEEK AT THE FF IN ACTION.
COURTNEY WOULD JUST DIE IF SHE COULD SEE YOU NOW.
SHE'S ALWAYS HAD AN ITCH FOR FRANKLIN RICHARDS.
TO TELL THE TRUTH... SO HAVE YOU!
AND HE'S EVEN CUTER IN PERSON!

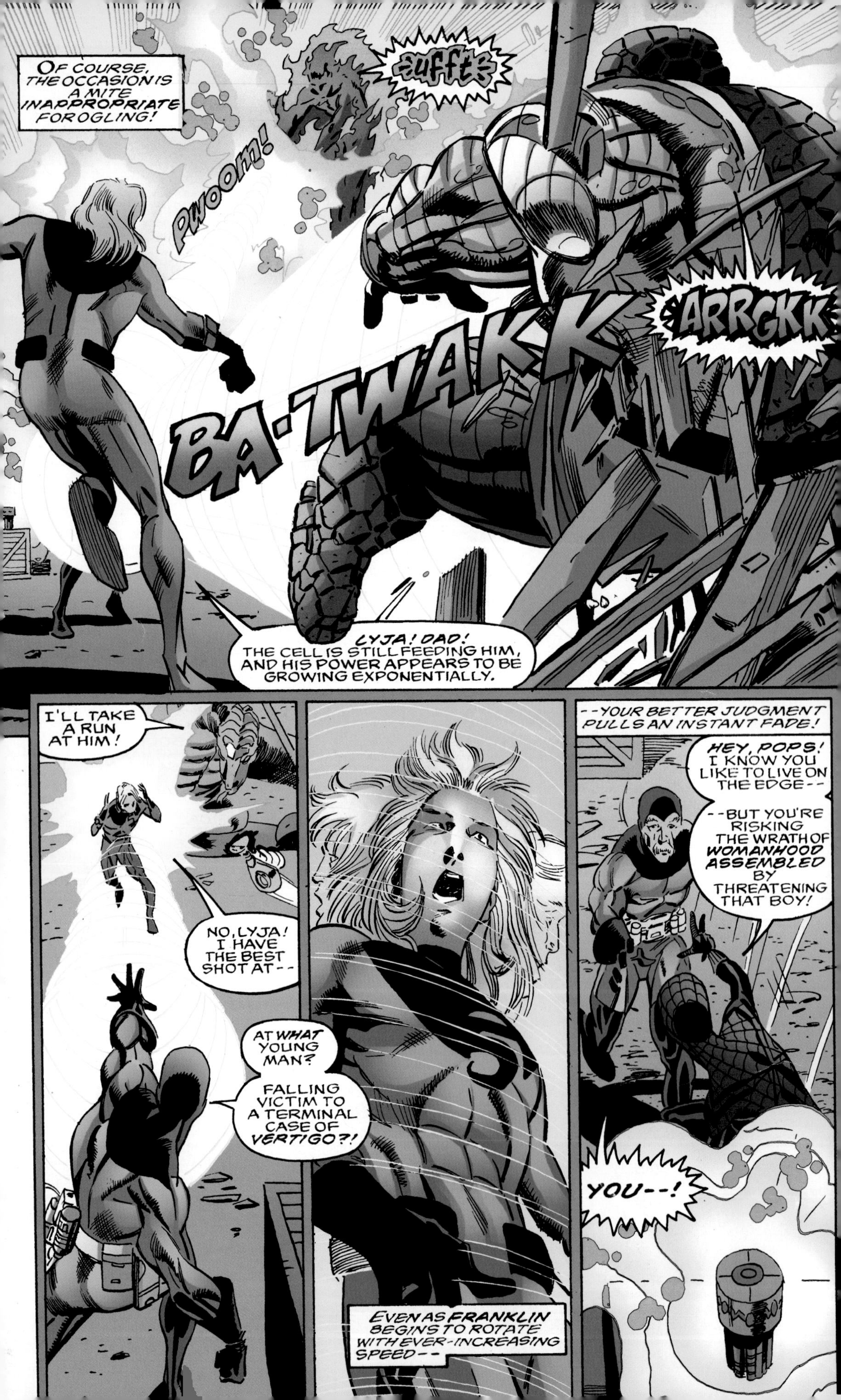

OF COURSE, THE OCCASION IS A MITE INAPPROPRIATE FOR OGLING!
-SUFFT-
PWOOM!
BA-TWAKK
ARRGKK
LYJA! DAD! THE CELL IS STILL FEEDING HIM, AND HIS POWER APPEARS TO BE GROWING EXPONENTIALLY.
I'LL TAKE A RUN AT HIM!
NO, LYJA! I HAVE THE BEST SHOT AT--
AT WHAT YOUNG MAN?
FALLING VICTIM TO A TERMINAL CASE OF VERTIGO?!
EVEN AS FRANKLIN BEGINS TO ROTATE WITH EVER-INCREASING SPEED--
--YOUR BETTER JUDGMENT PULLS AN INSTANT FADE!
HEY, POPS! I KNOW YOU LIKE TO LIVE ON THE EDGE--
--BUT YOU'RE RISKING THE WRATH OF WOMANHOOD ASSEMBLED BY THREATENING THAT BOY!
YOU--!

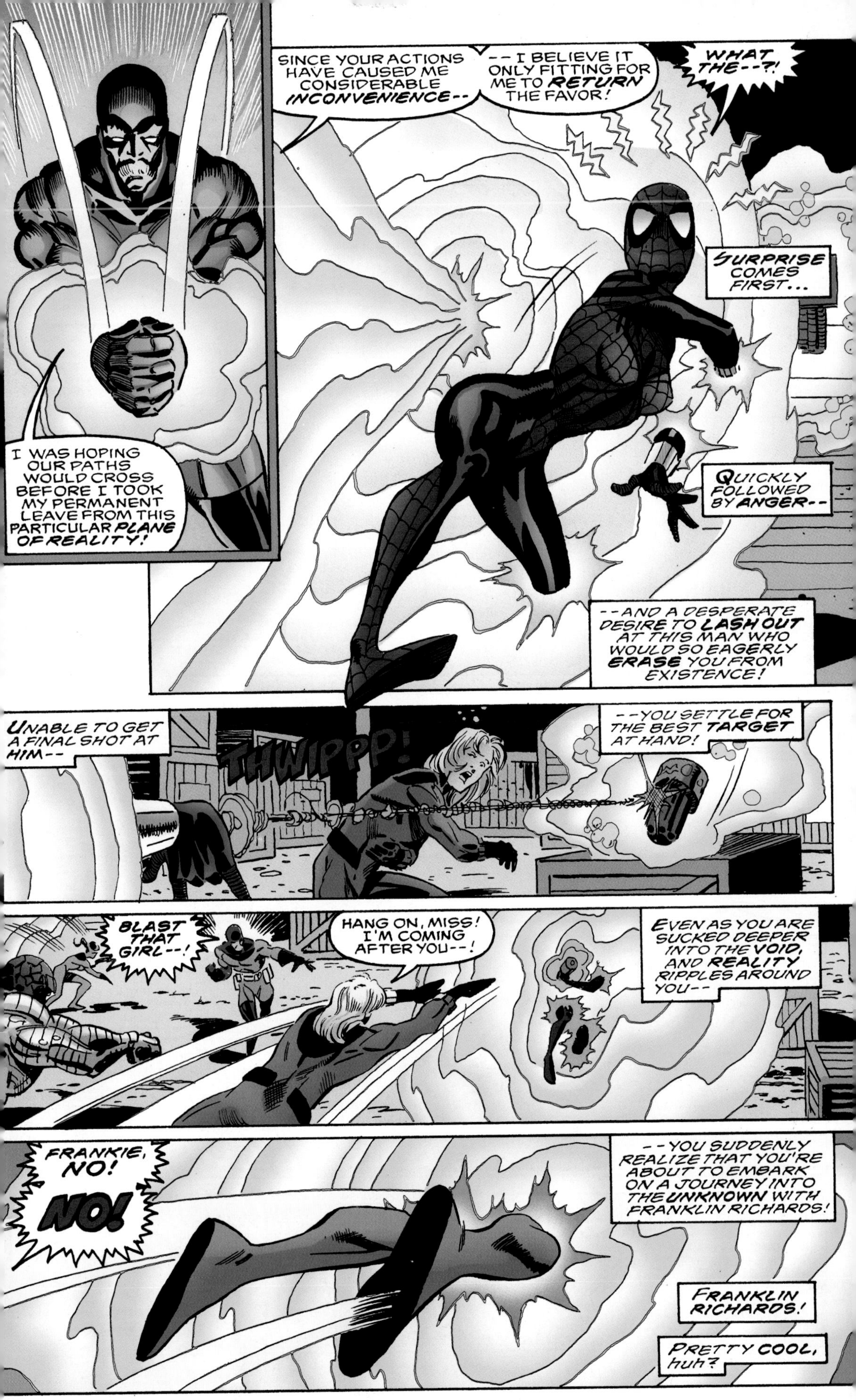

I WAS HOPING OUR PATHS WOULD CROSS BEFORE I TOOK MY PERMANENT LEAVE FROM THIS PARTICULAR PLANE OF REALITY!
SINCE YOUR ACTIONS HAVE CAUSED ME CONSIDERABLE INCONVENIENCE--
--I BELIEVE IT ONLY FITTING FOR ME TO RETURN THE FAVOR!
WHAT THE--?!
SURPRISE COMES FIRST...
QUICKLY FOLLOWED BY ANGER--
--AND A DESPERATE DESIRE TO LASH OUT AT THIS MAN WHO WOULD SO EAGERLY ERASE YOU FROM EXISTENCE!
UNABLE TO GET A FINAL SHOT AT HIM--
THWIPPP!
--YOU SETTLE FOR THE BEST TARGET AT HAND!
BLAST THAT GIRL--!
HANG ON, MISS! I'M COMING AFTER YOU--!
EVEN AS YOU ARE SUCKED DEEPER INTO THE VOID, AND REALITY RIPPLES AROUND YOU--
FRANKIE, NO!
NO!
--YOU SUDDENLY REALIZE THAT YOU'RE ABOUT TO EMBARK ON A JOURNEY INTO THE UNKNOWN WITH FRANKLIN RICHARDS!
FRANKLIN RICHARDS!
PRETTY COOL, huh?

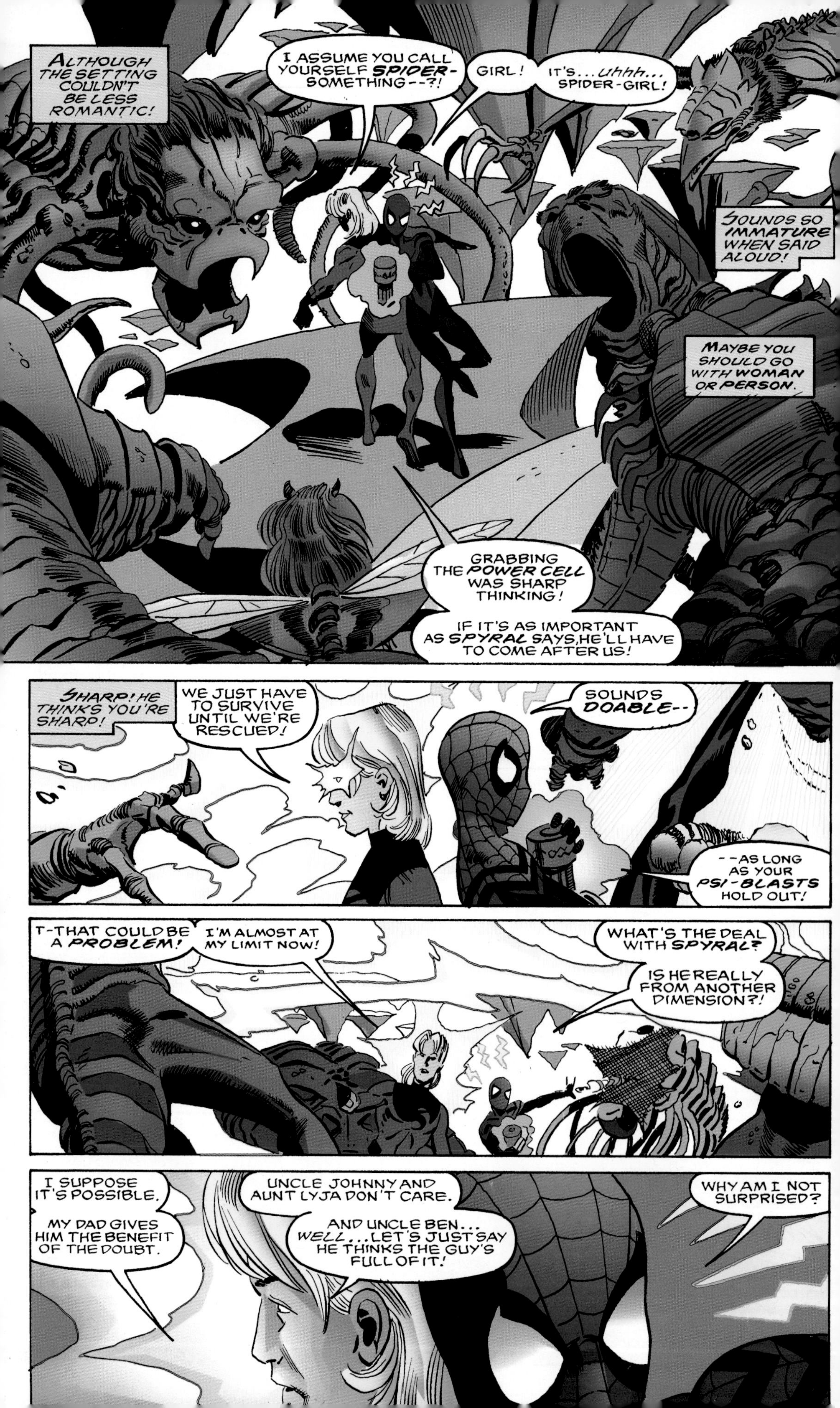
ALTHOUGH THE SETTING COULDN'T BE LESS ROMANTIC!
I ASSUME YOU CALL YOURSELF SPIDER-SOMETHING--?!
GIRL!
IT'S...uhhh... SPIDER-GIRL!
SOUNDS SO IMMATURE WHEN SAID ALOUD!
MAYBE YOU SHOULD GO WITH WOMAN OR PERSON.
GRABBING THE POWER CELL WAS SHARP THINKING!
IF IT'S AS IMPORTANT AS SPYRAL SAYS, HE'LL HAVE TO COME AFTER US!
SHARP! HE THINKS YOU'RE SHARP!
WE JUST HAVE TO SURVIVE UNTIL WE'RE RESCUED!
SOUNDS DOABLE--
--AS LONG AS YOUR PSI-BLASTS HOLD OUT!
T-THAT COULD BE A PROBLEM!
I'M ALMOST AT MY LIMIT NOW!
WHAT'S THE DEAL WITH SPYRAL?
IS HE REALLY FROM ANOTHER DIMENSION?!
I SUPPOSE IT'S POSSIBLE.
MY DAD GIVES HIM THE BENEFIT OF THE DOUBT.
UNCLE JOHNNY AND AUNT LYJA DON'T CARE.
AND UNCLE BEN... WELL... LET'S JUST SAY HE THINKS THE GUY'S FULL OF IT!
WHY AM I NOT SURPRISED?

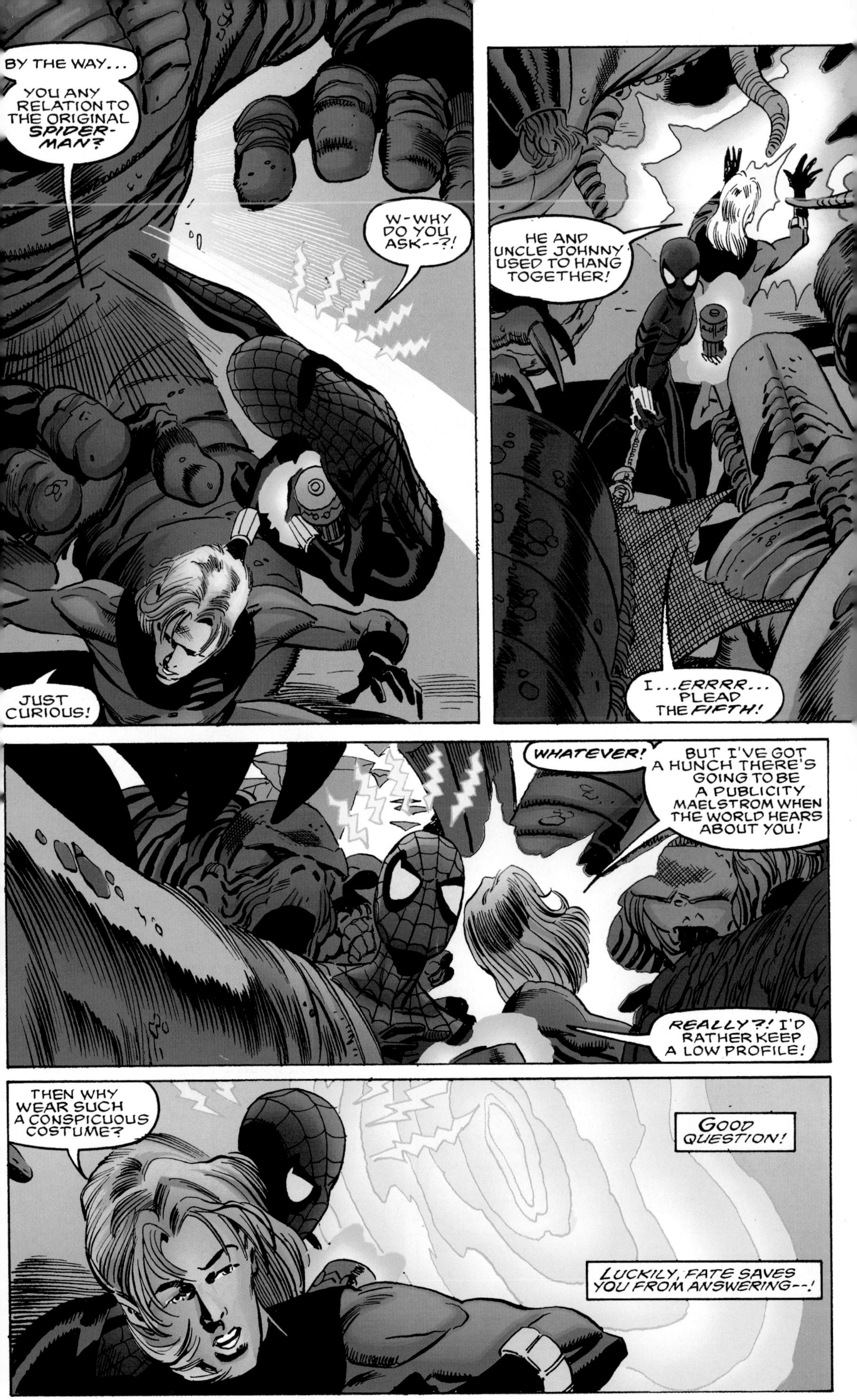
BY THE WAY...
YOU ANY RELATION TO THE ORIGINAL SPIDER-MAN?
W-WHY DO YOU ASK--?!
JUST CURIOUS!
HE AND UNCLE JOHNNY USED TO HANG TOGETHER!
I...ERRRR... PLEAD THE FIFTH!
WHATEVER!
BUT I'VE GOT A HUNCH THERE'S GOING TO BE A PUBLICITY MAELSTROM WHEN THE WORLD HEARS ABOUT YOU!
REALLY?! I'D RATHER KEEP A LOW PROFILE!
THEN WHY WEAR SUCH A CONSPICUOUS COSTUME?
GOOD QUESTION!
LUCKILY, FATE SAVES YOU FROM ANSWERING--!

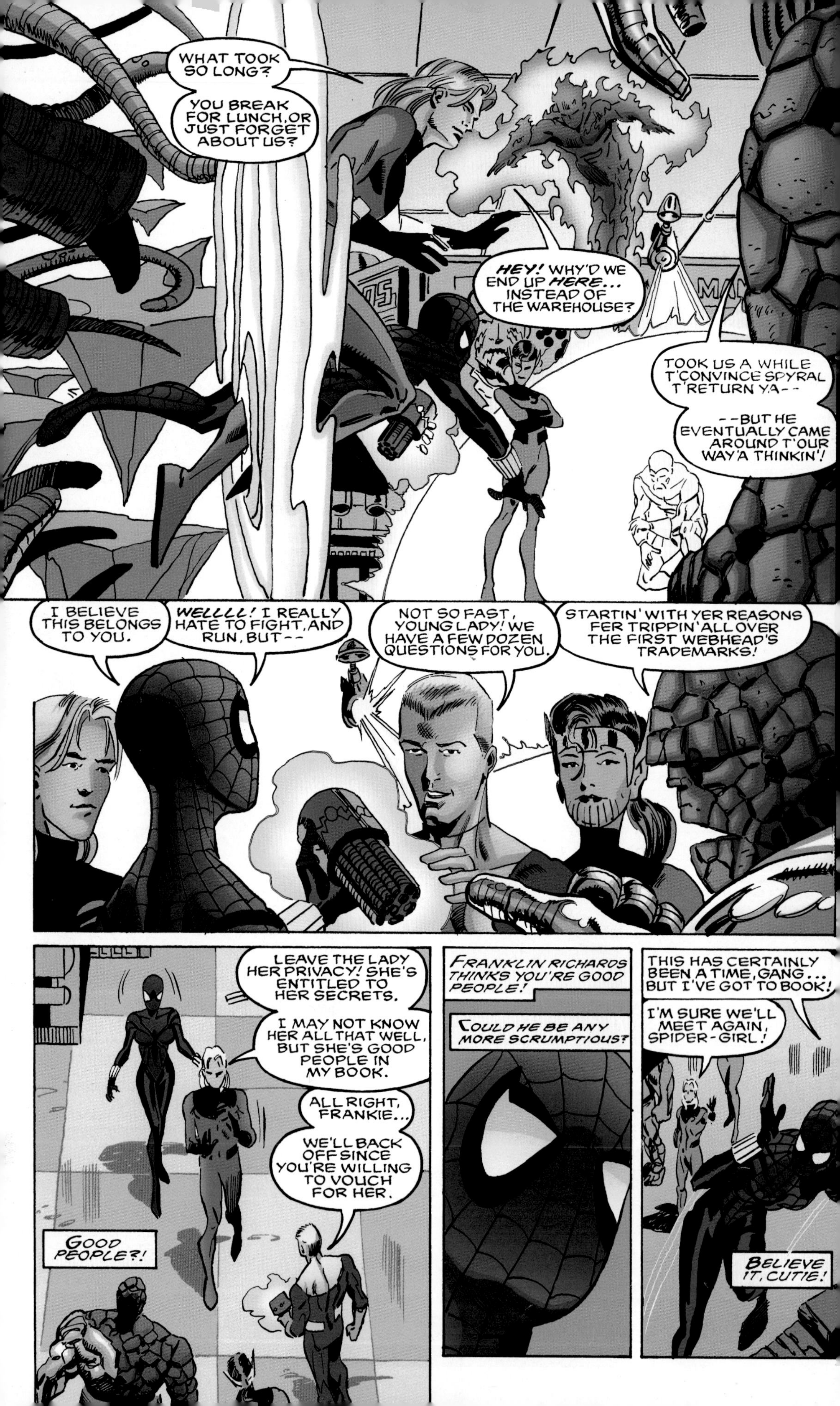
WHAT TOOK SO LONG?
YOU BREAK FOR LUNCH, OR JUST FORGET ABOUT US?
HEY! WHY'D WE END UP HERE... INSTEAD OF THE WAREHOUSE?
TOOK US A WHILE T'CONVINCE SPYRAL T'RETURN YA--
--BUT HE EVENTUALLY CAME AROUND T'OUR WAY'A THINKIN'!
I BELIEVE THIS BELONGS TO YOU.
WELLLL! I REALLY HATE TO FIGHT, AND RUN, BUT--
NOT SO FAST, YOUNG LADY! WE HAVE A FEW DOZEN QUESTIONS FOR YOU.
STARTIN' WITH YER REASONS FER TRIPPIN' ALL OVER THE FIRST WEBHEAD'S TRADEMARKS!
LEAVE THE LADY HER PRIVACY! SHE'S ENTITLED TO HER SECRETS.
I MAY NOT KNOW HER ALL THAT WELL, BUT SHE'S GOOD PEOPLE IN MY BOOK.
ALL RIGHT, FRANKIE...
WE'LL BACK OFF SINCE YOU'RE WILLING TO VOUCH FOR HER.
GOOD PEOPLE?!
FRANKLIN RICHARDS THINKS YOU'RE GOOD PEOPLE!
COULD HE BE ANY MORE SCRUMPTIOUS?
THIS HAS CERTAINLY BEEN A TIME, GANG... BUT I'VE GOT TO BOOK!
I'M SURE WE'LL MEET AGAIN, SPIDER-GIRL!
BELIEVE IT, CUTIE!

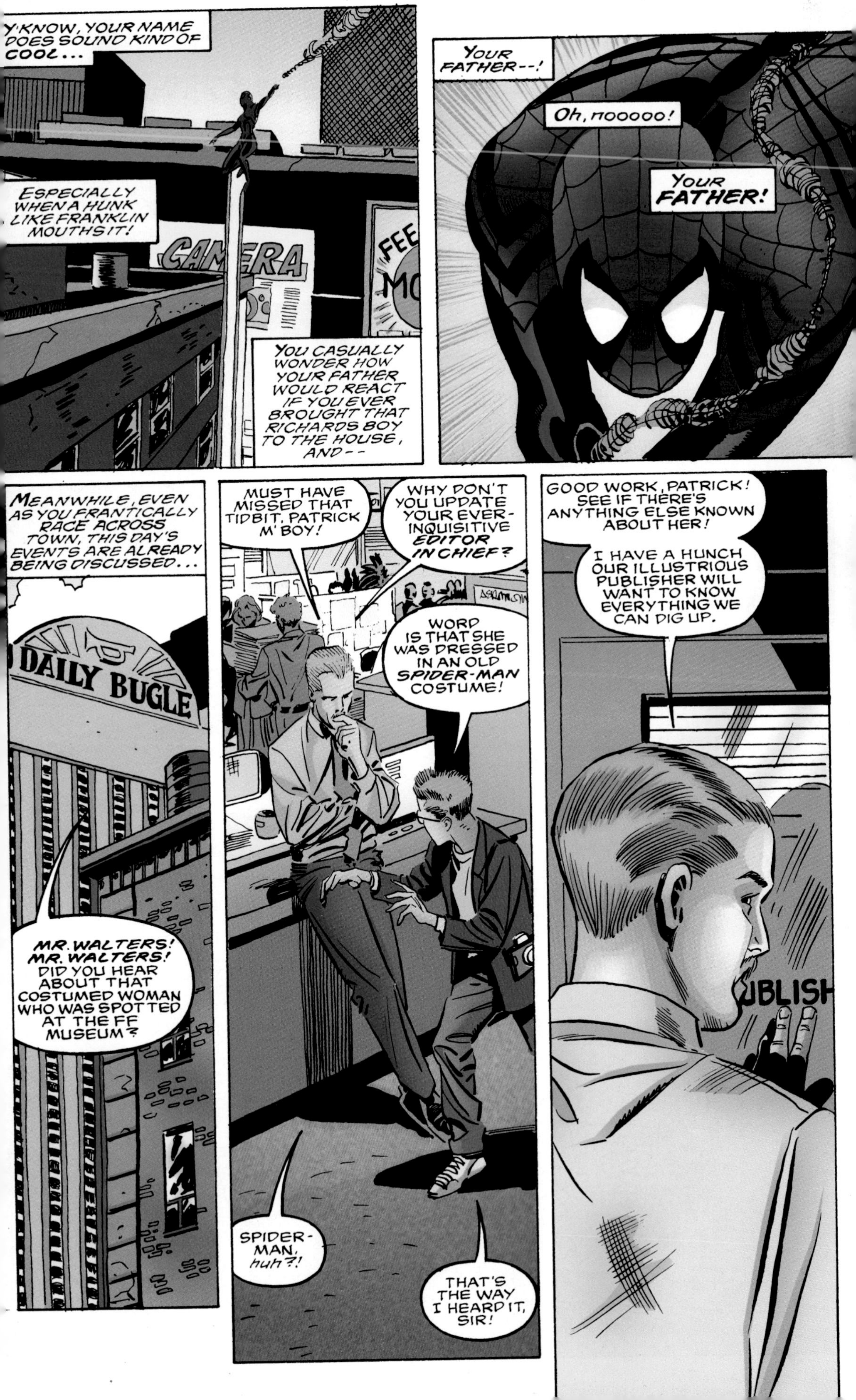

Y'KNOW, YOUR NAME DOES SOUND KIND OF COOL...
ESPECIALLY WHEN A HUNK LIKE FRANKLIN MOUTHS IT!
CAMERA
YOU CASUALLY WONDER HOW YOUR FATHER WOULD REACT IF YOU EVER BROUGHT THAT RICHARDS BOY TO THE HOUSE, AND--
YOUR FATHER--!
Oh, noooooo!
YOUR FATHER!
MEANWHILE, EVEN AS YOU FRANTICALLY RACE ACROSS TOWN, THIS DAY'S EVENTS ARE ALREADY BEING DISCUSSED...
DAILY BUGLE
MR. WALTERS! MR. WALTERS! DID YOU HEAR ABOUT THAT COSTUMED WOMAN WHO WAS SPOTTED AT THE FF MUSEUM?
MUST HAVE MISSED THAT TIDBIT, PATRICK M'BOY!
WHY DON'T YOU UPDATE YOUR EVER-INQUISITIVE EDITOR IN CHIEF?
WORD IS THAT SHE WAS DRESSED IN AN OLD SPIDER-MAN COSTUME!
SPIDER-MAN, huh?!
THAT'S THE WAY I HEARD IT, SIR!
GOOD WORK, PATRICK! SEE IF THERE'S ANYTHING ELSE KNOWN ABOUT HER!
I HAVE A HUNCH OUR ILLUSTRIOUS PUBLISHER WILL WANT TO KNOW EVERYTHING WE CAN DIG UP.
UBLISH

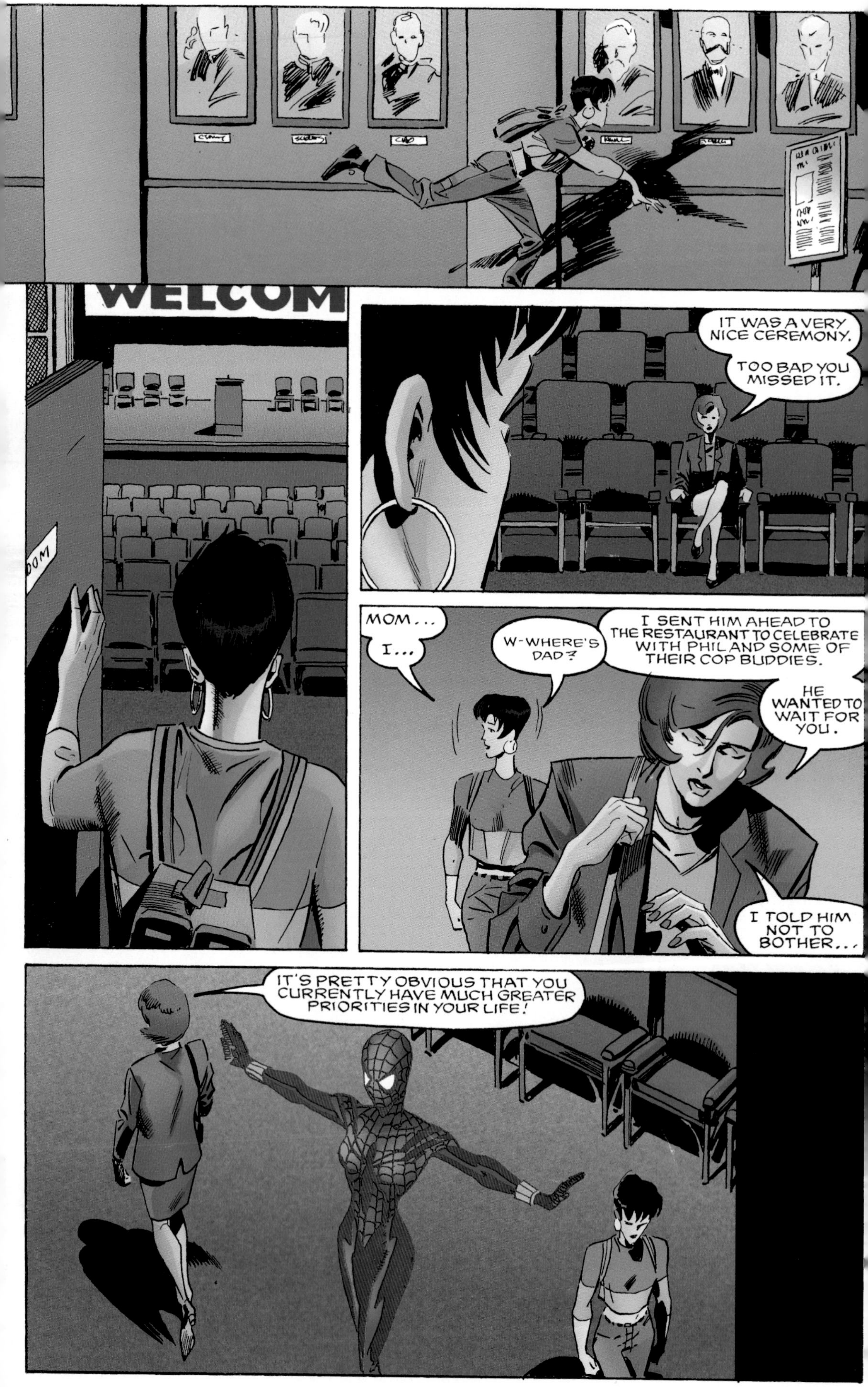
WELCOM
IT WAS A VERY NICE CEREMONY.
TOO BAD YOU MISSED IT.
MOM... I...
W-WHERE'S DAD?
I SENT HIM AHEAD TO THE RESTAURANT TO CELEBRATE WITH PHIL AND SOME OF THEIR COP BUDDIES.
HE WANTED TO WAIT FOR YOU.
I TOLD HIM NOT TO BOTHER...
IT'S PRETTY OBVIOUS THAT YOU CURRENTLY HAVE MUCH GREATER PRIORITIES IN YOUR LIFE!